FALLEN STAR

FALLEN STAR

Peter J. Falotico

CHAPTER 1

It was 8:30 a.m. on a warm spring day when Bobby Shane made his way out of the Pennsylvania Station onto 8th Avenue. He squinted in the bright sunlight, shading his eyes with his hand. He felt dwarfed by the awe-inspiring skyscrapers that towered above him. The early morning rush hour and the scent of sidewalk grills added to his excitement. The streets were jammed with automobile traffic; horns blared and tires squealed. Everyone was in a hurry as they rushed to their work places. Panhandlers lined the sidewalks, begging for whatever they could find.

In his peripheral vision, he saw a slender figure move toward him, disrupting his concentration. She was a young, well-endowed blonde who was wearing all black, from her leather jacket to the shiny boots over her fishnet stockings. Her black skirt stopped above her knees.

"Hi, honey. My name is Trudy, and for only a few dollars I can show you a good time—one you'll never forget. How about it, handsome?"

"No thanks. I'm not in the mood now. It's too early. Let me have your name and telephone number and I'll call you when I'm ready for a good time."

"You trying to be a wise guy, mister?" She abruptly turned and walked away, looking for her next opportunity.

He decided to have breakfast in a diner across the street; then he would look for lodging. He'd had little to eat since he left Cincinnati on the all-night train. Dashing across the intersection, he almost collided with a cab, drawing derogatory remarks from the driver.

"Ah, up yours!" he yelled in return as he entered the diner. He ordered two eggs over easy, bacon, toast, home fries, and coffee.

* * *

Without a thought about cost, he checked into a comfortable hotel.

"That'll be ninety dollars a night, sir, plus taxes," the clerk informed him.

Too embarrassed to cancel, he thought to himself *you'd better get your behind out tomorrow morning and find something cheaper.*

Check-in was inconveniently scheduled at two o'clock. With over three hours to spare, he visited historic 42nd and Broadway, which was just a short distance from the hotel. He was impressed by the sights of this great metropolis as he walked down the street once roamed by the greats: Ziegfield, Cohen, and Rogers and Hammerstein.

He stopped at a newsstand and bought a paper. He returned to the hotel and scoured the classifieds, hoping to find theatrical agents seeking clients.

After two o'clock, he checked into his room and took a much-needed shower. He lay on the bed with the newspaper he intended to read, but soon dozed off.

By the shadows on the walls, he knew he had slept past dinnertime. He dressed himself and left his room for the lounge. Happy hour was still in progress: drinks were at half price, and the all-you-can-eat hors d'oeuvres were free. He sat at the bar and ordered a bourbon and ginger.

His attention was drawn to a young man singing at the piano in the far corner of the lounge. Impressed with his style, he moved closer to get a better listen. During a break in the set, he introduced himself.

"Hi, I'm Bobby Shane. I'm in New York for the first time, tackling a professional singing career. You sound great."

"Thanks for the compliment. I'm Jim Branton." They shook hands. "I'm always happy to meet a fellow singer. Do you have an agent?"

"No, but I'll be searching for one in the next few days."

"Locating an agent will be your biggest challenge. There are a million singers in New York looking for agents and jobs. Most strike out. I'm lucky because I play the piano. It makes it easier to find work."

Bobby self-confidence slipped a couple of notches.

"Break's over. I have to get back to work. Tell you what, stick around until I finish my final set and we'll chat awhile."

"Sure why not." Bobby answered.

Jim went back to entertaining the customers. Bobby found a small round table and nursed his bourbon. Looking down into his drink, he concentrated on Jim's singing, hoping to learn something.

With his final set completed, Jim joined Bobby and ordered a sandwich and a drink. "So, Bobby, tell me a little about yourself."

"Well, I was born and raised in Cincinnati. After graduating from high school, I worked as an accounting clerk for a bank, but I always enjoyed singing. I began singing at weddings and various parties. A few of my friends would light up my ego and tell me how great I was and that I should pursue a singing career. So coming to New York seemed like a good idea, but I needed the finances. My mother and father passed away before I was twenty. I decided to sell the house, which still had a mortgage. When all was said and done, I netted fourteen thousand dollars—that's what I'm living on right now. Hopefully I can find something to supplement my savings until I can find a singing job."

"Have you ever sung professionally or had any lessons?"

"None. As I said earlier, many of my friends felt that I would be able to succeed as a singer! It was then that I decided to go pro.

Jim appeared skeptical. "I hope your friends were right."

*　　*　　*

Early the next morning, Bobby checked out of the hotel and began searching for an apartment. He found several to his liking, but the prices were beyond his means. He was ready to give up when he noticed a shingle hanging on the door of a 3rd Avenue brownstone: ROOMS FOR RENT BY THE WEEK/MONTH—Mr C. Slade, Superintendent.

This might work, he thought as he knocked on the door.

A short, gray-haired gentleman answered the door.

"Mr. Slade?"

"Yes, I'm Mr. Slade. What can I do for you?"

"I've been looking for a furnished apartment and I saw your sign."

"I may have just the room for you." His eyes disappeared when he smiled. "Follow me and I'll show you. It's one room and a bath."

Bobby followed the landlord up two flights of stairs before they reached the apartment. The door opened to a bright one room dwelling with an adjacent bathroom. The necessities were on display: a sofa and chair, a table and lamp in the living area of the room. Toward the back, he saw a bed, a lamp and nightstand, and a television on a stand.

"Good," he said. "What's the cost?"

"Seven hundred dollars a week, two weeks in advance. There is no cooking and no women after dark. Married?"

"No, I'm single. And I'll take it."

"What do you do for a living?"

"I'm a singer," he answered proudly as he counted out fourteen hundred dollars.

Mr. Slade put the money in his pocket and wished him luck.

"If there is anything that I can do for you, knock on my door anytime."

*   *   *

Bobby took a break from unpacking and read the show business section of the paper he had purchased earlier in the day. He opened a phone book to the Agents listing and jotted down a few names and addresses.

*   *   *

At eight o'clock, Bobby was ready to look for an agent. He tucked his portfolio of sheet music under his arm and hit the city streets.

His first encounter with an agent was short and to-the-point. They weren't interested. *Strike one*, Bobby counted.

On 48th Street he entered a large, elegantly furnished office. He approached a young brunette who was typing diligently.

"Hi, can I help you?"

"My name is Bobby Shane. I'm a singer looking for an agent."

"Please be seated, Mr. Shane." She rose from her seat and disappeared into an adjacent office. She emerged a few moments later.

"Mr. Ryan will see you now, Mr. Shane." She led Bobby into the office.

Mr. Ryan stared at Bobby while he fiddled with his pencil. "Well now, you're a singer?"

"Yes," Bobby replied nervously.

"Any experience, Mr. Shane?"

"I sang in Cincinnati," Bobby said without elaborating.

"Did you sing professionally?" Mr. Ryan twirled a pencil between his fingers as he waited on Bobby's answer.

"No."

"I'm sorry, Mr. Shane. I don't have a need for singers at the present time. Check with me in a month or so—by then I may have something."

Strike two. Damn, not even an audition. He'd been in New York only two days; now he wondered if he had made a mistake trying to break into show business on the world's biggest stage. As he searched for another agency, the city blocks seemed to be getting longer.

He entered the well-kept offices of the Howard and Wayne Agency. He approached the secretary and spilled his practiced line.

"I'm a singer looking for an agent."

"Do you have an appointment?"

"No." Thinking it was another lost cause, he turned to leave.

"One moment, sir." She picked up the telephone and spoke with someone in another office. "Have a seat, Mr. Shane. Mr. Howard will be with you shortly."

Thirty minutes later, he was given another chance to sell himself.

"Mr. Shane, I'm Edward Howard. What can I do for you?"

"I'm a singer, Mr. Howard. I know that an entertainer needs an agent to get into show business, and I'm hoping you could get me started in my singing career."

"Have you gotten good reviews?"

"I believe so. Back home, I was asked to sing at local social affairs."

"Well, right now I have a full compliment of singers. Come in Thursday around ten and I'll listen to you. If you have what it takes, I'll see what I can do. No promises, mind you."

Bobby felt a lot better this time. Even with a feeling of accomplishment, he pressed on with his search. He didn't get past the secretaries of the next three agencies. Appointments were needed, professional experience a must. Despite being drained and disappointed, he wasn't giving up. The yellow pages yielded a few more leads.

*　　*　　*

It was Thursday morning, and Bobby was anxious to get to his audition for Mr. Howard. He leapt up the stairs two-at-a-time to Mr. Howard's offices.

"Good morning. I'm Bobby Shane. I have an appointment with Mr. Howard," he said cheerfully.

"I'm sorry, Mr. Shane, but Mr. Howard had to go out of town on emergency business and I'm not certain when he will return."

"Mr. Howard is out of town on business?" His heart sunk to the floor. "Okay, how about Mr. Wayne?"

"He's on vacation for the next two weeks."

It was a mighty blow. He felt it would have been better had Mr. Howard turned him down when they first met. With his hopes deflated, he stared into Margaret's sympathetic eyes.

"It's not your fault," he assured her. "Thank you anyway."

*   *   *

By now he had exhausted every agent listed in the yellow pages except for one: M. Edelstein Agency. He entered a second floor office and saw a man reclining in a high-back chair behind a plush mahogany desk.

"Mr. Edelstein?"

"No, I'm Mr. Silverman," he chuckled as he pulled himself closer to the desk. "I took over the business from Mat Edelstein, and I've been too busy to change the sign. What can I do for you Mr.—?"

"Bobby Shane." He extended his hand in greeting and continued, "I'm a singer looking for an agent."

"This may be your lucky day, Mr. Shane." He looked down at his watch. "They should be there now." Mr. Silverman took a business card from its holder and scribbled a note on the reverse side. "Take this card to the Holstein's Dinner Theater on 48th Street and give it to Max Bloom. There's a band scheduled to play there for the next six months. They're holding an open audition for singers. If you can pass it, you have a job. Then you can come back to my office and we'll discuss a contract."

"Great!" Bobby quickly shook Silverman's hand and then left for the dinner theater.

He entered the building through the employees' entrance that led to a stage where a band was rehearsing. He asked the first person he met for Max Bloom. The stranger pointed to two men sitting at the edge of the stage.

"Max Bloom?"

"I'm Max. What can I do for you?"

Bobby introduced himself and handed him Silverman's business card. Max turned the card over. "Bobby Shane, eh?"

"Yes," he replied quickly. Max introduced him to Frank Martin, the bandleader. Frank called out, "George, this is Bobby Shane. He's here for an audition."

"Do you have arrangements?" George asked.

"Yes," Bobby answered as he fumbled for his sheet music.

George sat at the piano and played a few bars from the sheet Bobby had given him. "Okay, on three—one, two, three."

Bobby began singing, but his voice quavered. Frank turned to Max halfway through the number. His bushy eyebrows came together in a frown as he whispered, "You need to have a talk with Silverman. We need an experienced singer, not an amateur."

"Yeah, I'll talk to him tonight," Max answered, slightly upset at the disruption in his schedule.

When Bobby finished his song, Max announced, "Thanks, Mr. Shane. We appreciate you coming in. You'll hear from Mr. Silverman in a few days."

Dejected, Bobby walked toward the exit, aware of his failure. Outside of the theater, he noticed a teenager talking on a public phone. He was immediately reminded that he hadn't called Mary since he arrived. He had promised her he would call when he got to New York. He dashed to a phone. "Operator, a collect call please to Mary Rich, Cincinnati Ohio, number—"

Mary Rich was an only child like Bobby, and only one year his junior. She was an intelligent woman who always kept herself impeccably groomed. She had shiny black hair and deep brown eyes that were framed by long, wet eyelashes. She was a warm, generous person who could make easy conversation with anyone. And she loved Bobby. But his love for her was strictly platonic.

"Mary? Hi, I'm here in New York. I'm calling you from a phone booth in Times Square! Sorry that I didn't call sooner, but I've been running around interviewing with various agents."

"I can imagine. Any luck so far?"

"Not yet, but I have a few interested agents, and will be auditioning for two of them this week. How is everyone? How's your mom and dad?"

"They're fine, thank you. Did you find a nice place to live?"

"Yes, a great place in downtown Manhattan on 31st Street and 3rd Avenue."

"That's nice. I miss you, Bobby." She spoke her words quietly so that her parents wouldn't hear.

"Well Mary, I don't want to run up your phone bill, so I'll close for now. I'll call you in a few days, hopefully with good news, okay?"

"All right. Good luck, Bobby."

He bought the newspaper on his way to his apartment to look for a temporary job. He noticed that the entertainment section featured clubs in Greenwich Village, and jotted down a few prospects.

*   *   *

The next morning, he visited an insurance company. Although the ad stated that a high school diploma was the minimum requirement, he could tell they were really looking for a college graduate. He was rejected by the second company on his list because he had no prior experience in sales. The third on the list seemed easy—a parking garage attendant at Gilliam's' Garage, nine dollars an hour. He filled out the application and was instructed to report at eight o'clock the next morning to meet the manager. He didn't mention that he hadn't driven a car for a few years. He'd driven Mary's father's car on occasion, but his driver's license had since expired.

*   *   *

Bobby took a bus to Greenwich Village, where he visited four cabarets, but they only dealt with agents. As he was heading to catch a bus back to his apartment, he found a small out-of-the-way club. *What do I have to lose? I'll give it a try.*

An elderly gentleman was cleaning a window that read Morgan's Ale House in green letters.

"Excuse me—would you know if there is anyone in there?"

"Yeah, there's somebody in there." The old man paid him little attention. He picked up a large sponge and continued to wash the window.

"Uh, the reason I ask is that I'm looking for a job, and I thought I might speak with someone."

"He needs no help. He's got me."

"No, I'm looking for a *singing* job."

"Well, that's different. Mr. Morgan should be in his office."

"May I?" He gestured for the man to step aside.

The club stunk of stale cigarette and cigar smoke from the night before. The room looked big enough to accommodate about seventy-five patrons. It had a ten-foot by fifteen-foot hardwood dance floor, but there wasn't anything resembling a stage. Bobby saw a black upright piano tucked in a corner. In a tiny room at the far end of the bar, Bobby saw a man who looked to be in his late forties. He was wearing a sweatshirt, blue jeans, and sneakers. He sat at a makeshift Plexiglas desk, working feverishly on the last night's receipts.

"Mr. Morgan?"

"Yes, I'm Mr. Morgan. How did you get in here? And what can I do for you?"

Bobby smiled and spoke quickly. "My name is Bobby Shane. I'm looking for a singing job. I like to make people happy by singing to them. I also need a daytime job so I can pay my expenses. I found the day job at Gilliam's garage, but I'm having a hell of a time finding someone who needs a singer. I passed your club on the way to the bus stop and thought maybe I'd take a chance and get lucky. I asked the window cleaner if anyone was in here, and he mentioned that I'd find you in your office."

"Whoa," Morgan answered as he rolled his eyes. "I need to have a talk with him. As you can see, this is a small club, primarily for local folks who like to sit and chat, enjoy a drink and a sandwich. I don't feature much entertainment except a piano player on Saturday nights and a jukebox during the week."

Morgan paused for a moment and then continued, "You know, Mr. Shane, you made me think of something. A singer might enhance my business. I'll hire you strictly on a trial basis. Morgan took a chance by not auditioning Bobby. If it works out and I make money, you have a job. I'll pay you a hundred dollars a night Wednesday, Friday, and Saturday evenings from nine to twelve, with a fifteen-minute break on the hour. No contract. If things don't work out, I need to be able to let you go at a moment's notice."

"You're on Mr. Morgan. When do I start?"

"Friday night. Be here at eight. I'll notify my piano player to make certain that he can work those nights."

Bobby thanked him and sealed the deal with a handshake.

"By the way, Mr. Shane—don't quit your day job."

Bobby threw his head back and smiled. "I won't—and thanks again."

*   *   *

The next morning he reported to his new job at Gilliam's Garage. It was a six-level indoor parking facility. The friendly materials' manager named Butch handed him the uniform he was required to wear: a pair of tan trousers, a shirt with the business logo stitched across the back, and a nametag for his breast pocket. Bobby's job seemed simple: parking cars when they were driven in, and delivering them to customers who were leaving. He would be partnered with Ed, an experienced employee, until he learned the routine. Although a little shaky, he survived the morning rush hour with Ed's help. However, the afternoon rush hour was different story—many cars were parked on the upper levels of the garage, and he had a problem navigating cars down the sharply angled exit ramp. He drove cautiously, but it was causing delays for the customers, who were becoming irate. Bobby developed a headache and was happy when six o'clock rolled around.

Arriving home, he removed his uniform and took a shower. He went to the closet and examined his tuxedo—it was in decent condition.

*   *   *

Friday evening, Bobby arrived at the club promptly at eight. Morgan introduced him to his piano player, Lester Brown. Lester was a gray-haired gentleman in his late seventies, with a little paunch around the middle. His wrinkled face told the story of a hard life. He was cordial and seemed receptive to being the accompanist.

After they rehearsed a few songs that would be featured that evening, Bobby stood at the bar, observing patrons as they wondered in. By nine o'clock the club was short of being full. It had become noisy and the cigarette and cigar smoke had already filled the air. Morgan asked the customers for their attention.

"Ladies and Gentleman, Morgan's Ale House is proud to announce that, beginning tonight, we'll be presenting live entertainment Wednesdays, Fridays, and Saturdays for your listening and dancing pleasure. Without further adieu, it is with great pleasure that I present the pride of Cincinnati, Ohio, the one and only, BOBBY SHANE!"

Bobby felt his heart race as he stepped up to the microphone and Lester arpeggiated an introduction. Initially, the audience gave him a cool reception. Two songs later, their din filled the room. For the most part, he was totally ignored. After each song, one or two patrons applauded, but he didn't receive the thunderclaps he had hoped to hear. He finished singing his last number, took an unseen bow, and sat next to Lester.

"A tough opening night." Lester remarked.

"That's a nice way of putting it, Lester. Was I bad? Was it stage fright?"

"Is this your first gig?"

"It showed, didn't it?"

"If you want the truth, you ain't ready for no big time. You need to find someone to coach you. You have a good voice, but it has got to be developed. Just having the fundamentals ain't enough to make the big time."

"Developed? What do you mean by developed?"

"If you don't mind me telling you, singing ain't just sound coming from the vocal cords. It's an art—stomach control, breathing, concentration."

"You seem to know about that. Can you help me develop, Lester?"

"I think I can. I'll give it a try. Be here an hour early tomorrow night and we'll begin training. If you're a quick learner, and with practice, it shouldn't take you long."

"Thanks, Lester. See you tomorrow night at eight."

*   *   *

The buzz of the alarm clock sent Bobby into a panic. He leaned over to see the time. It was eight-fifteen. Shit, *I'm going to be late for work.*

Bobby jumped right in with the rest of the crew. He was slow and still having problems navigating the vehicles from the upper levels. When the morning rush hour was over, the crew took a coffee break. Bobby sat next to Ed, and they began exchanging their personal histories. Ed told Bobby his combat stories about his girlfriends—single and married—and he enjoyed listening to every minute of it. Ed invited Bobby to meet a few of his friends and have a few brews a local tavern.

Bobby thanked him and told him that he might take him up on the offer sometime. Ed mentioned that the boss noticed a few irate customers yesterday. He reminded him to try and hustle. Bobby thanked him and walked to the garage entrance to wait for the next customer.

The late rush hour began. Bobby took a deep breath, accepted a ticket from a customer, and retrieved the keys from the cashier. With no end to Bobby's bad luck, he discovered the vehicle was parked on the sixth level. He quickly scampered up the ramp, thinking that it would be faster than the elevator. He was wrong; he ended up losing thirty to forty seconds.

As he proceeded down the exit ramp, the walls seemed to close in on him. When he finally arrived at street level, the customer asked him if he had a valid drivers license. Bobby ignored him and went to the cashier for the next pickup.

Ed realized that Bobby had a problem with the ramp and that he was an inexperienced driver. He was behind Bobby as he stood at the cashier's booth and picked up the next set of keys for a car parked on the fifth level.

"Ah, hell," Bobby said when he noticed the location.

Ed asked Bobby for the keys. "I'll take this one and every other car above the second level. You take the cars located on the first and second levels."

Unfortunately for Bobby, most of the cars were located in the higher levels. Having no choice, he struggled throughout the rush hour. By day's end, Bobby had served four irate customers. They complained about him taking too much time. The boss was about to reprimand him when Ed explained that Bobby was still learning, and that he would improve in no time.

"He'd better or he's out—do you understand?"

"Yes, sir, I understand."

Bobby and Ed left the garage together.

"Thanks for helping me out, Ed."

"My pleasure. A few more days of driving these cars, and you'll get the hang of it."

"I hope so."

Ed invited Bobby for a drink at a local bar called Joey's.

"Sure, why not? But I can only stay for an hour or so."

They entered a smoky bar filled with people enjoying the happy hour. Everyone in the place seemed to know Ed. Ed introduced Bobby to a few friends sitting at a large table, then they sat down. Ed ordered a beer for himself and then looked at Bobby.

"Oh, bourbon and ginger on the rocks, please."

Their conversation hit the usual subjects: the latest jokes, who didn't like the boss, their jobs.

Suddenly, Bobby's attention was drawn to one of the waitresses. The nametag on her white blouse read "Sandy". Her tight-fitting short black skirt highlighted her shapely legs. Her brunette tresses were tied back and clamped in place with a huge barrette. As she looked over to Bobby, their eyes locked. Bobby felt a chill up and down his spine.

She approached the table and asked if anyone required a refill. She focused her eyes directly onto Bobby's. Ed ordered another round. She turned and walked to the bar, swaying all the way. As she waited for the drinks, she turned her head sideways and stared at Bobby. For the next few minutes, Sandy did all she could to get Bobby's attention.

Ed noticed what was happening and began to worry. He knew that Sandy was the girlfriend of the owner, who just happened to be at the bar observing Bobby and Sandy.

As he started walking in Bobby's direction, Ed stood up and met him halfway. They talked for a few minutes and then walked back to the bar.

Ed returned and whispered the situation to Bobby. They continued drinking and conversing for a little while longer. Bobby glanced at his watch—it was seven o'clock. He had only an hour to change, get to the club, and work with Lester for his singing lesson.

He stood up and thanked Ed, shook the hands of his companions, and headed for home.

*   *   *

When Bobby arrived at Morgan's Ale House, Lester was waiting with a cigarette in one hand and a cup of coffee in the other.

"Hi, Lester."

"Hi yourself. Ready to get to work?" Lester went on to explain what he meant by the art of controlling the voice through breathing and stomach muscle control. He had Bobby doing scales for the next twenty minutes. The breathing and stomach control exercises made his stomach ache.

"That's it for now. It's almost show time. We'll go at it again Wednesday night." Lester gave him a list of stomach and breathing exercises to do at home.

The evening ended the same as the previous evening had. Bobby hurried home to his apartment and immediately began practicing. He practiced until three in the morning, when the tenants complained.

*   *   *

The morning rush hour at Gilliam's went by without incident. However, the evening rush hour was a different story. The first customer Bobby encountered was the hard-nosed bastard who had given him hell about taking so long getting his car the night before. To make matters worse, the car was parked on the fifth level. Bobby ran to the elevator, taking it to the fifth level. In his haste, he drove the car down too quickly, and scraped its right side against the concrete barrier. The manager did all he could to quell the disturbance, telling the customer the he would pay for the necessary repairs.

The manager fired Bobby. Bobby understood and thanked him for opportunity.

On the way out, Ed shook his hand and wished him well.

*   *   *

It was Wednesday evening, and Bobby found Lester waiting for him at the piano.

"All right, let's see if you've been practicing." He played the introduction to "Somewhere". As Bobby sang, Lester grinned with approval. "You're getting it. You're getting better."

At show time, Bobby noticed that the audience seemed a little more appreciative, and he wondered if it was just coincidence or if his voice was really improving under Lester's tutelage. *Nah, it has to be coincidence— a different night, a different crowd.* With his last song finished, he sat next to Lester. "I really appreciate what you're doing for me, and I won't forget it."

"My pleasure. Remember, you must always make time for practice. You know the old saying, Practice makes perfect. And don't let the audience dictate to you. You dictate to the audience."

"I'll remember Lester. I'll remember."

*   *   *

Bobby slept until late Sunday morning. He wanted to rest and then treat himself to a full course dinner, but he ended up practicing for two hours. He had made an early dinner reservation at a restaurant on 43rd Street. After his meal, he went to the movies. By seven o'clock, he arrived back home. He kicked off his shoes, removed his tie, and tuned in to soft music on the radio. He was about to relax when he heard a knock on his door. Thinking that it was Slade, he hurried to open the door. There stood Sandy, the waitress from Joey's bar. Bobby stood speechless and pleasantly surprised.

"Well, don't just stand there. Aren't you going to invite me in?"

"Sure, sure. Come in."

She sat on the couch and Bobby took a seat on a chair directly across from her.

"How did you-?"

"Find you? I just happen to have a friend who is the bookkeeper at the parking garage. She was nice enough to furnish me with your address."

Her beauty mesmerized Bobby. He felt the blood rush to his head with the thought of how this evening could end. He offered to buy her a drink at a local pub, a few blocks away.

"I would love to."

Bobby put on his tie and coat back on and they left for the bar. Although Sandy had brought her car, they decided to walk. At the pub, they listened to the music as she sipped a Manhattan. He never thought that seeing her again was possible. Getting Ed in trouble was the furthest from his mind. For the next hour, they ate pizza and talked. When they were finished eating, they returned to Bobby's place.

Bobby led the way up the front steps, shielding Sandy in case Slade might be looking out the window. Once inside his apartment, they made love. Afterward, Sandy dressed and was preparing to leave. Bobby tried to persuade her to stay the night, but was unsuccessful. He escorted her to her car, again making sure that Slade was not around. She thanked him for a lovely evening. Without mentioning a next time, she left. Bobby felt a sense of masculine accomplishment.

Bobby was up early Monday morning looking for a day job. It was as bad as it had been looking for an agent. On his way home, he purchased a newspaper. He ate at a local deli, returned home, and fell asleep while listening to soft music emanating from the radio.

*   *   *

Over the next eleven weeks, Lester's coaching seemed to be bearing fruit. More patrons showed up at Bobby's performances, which made Morgan happy.

*   *   *

One month later, on a Wednesday evening, Bobby arrived at the club as usual. But Lester was nowhere to be found. Bobby sat at the piano, nervously tinkering with the keys. Lester was never late. As nine o'clock neared, Bobby decided to check with Morgan. In his office sat a sullen-faced Morgan, leaning back in his chair, and resting his folded hands behind his head.

"Hey, Morgan, what's up? Where's Lester?"

"Oh. Hi ya, Bobby. I have bad news."

"Hell, it can't be that bad, can it? I can take it." He braced himself.

"It's Lester." Morgan's eyes filled with tears.

"What about Lester?" Bobby tensed up.

"Lester passed away Monday evening."

"What? No! How?"

"A massive heart attack—as he slept. He went to bed and—" Morgan's voice trailed off.

After a long pause, Bobby said, "Well at least he didn't suffer. What about funeral arrangements?"

"Tomorrow morning, ten o'clock at Anderson's funeral parlor at 163rd Street. Lester had no family or insurance that I know of, so a few friends and I chipped in to pay for the funeral. It was the best we could afford."

"I would like to go along with you to the funeral."

"Of course, no problem." Morgan arranged to pick him up at his apartment at nine. One more thing." Morgan hesitated for a second. "I can't keep you on any longer. I was only paying Lester the minimum. For me to go out and get someone else would be too expensive. So it's back to the jukebox for now. Sorry, son."

"Mr. Morgan, I understand. I thank you for giving me the opportunity,"

He started to leave, but stopped at the piano. Staring at it, he sat and tinkered with the keys. He fought back tears as he thought *how could I have become so attached to someone after only knowing him for a short time?*

As he walked to the bus stop, he was deep in thought, remembering Lester. Not only did he lose a good friend, he lost his job.

*   *   *

Anderson's Funeral Home was crowded with many of Lester's friends—mostly musicians and patrons. There appeared to be no relatives present. A short, thin man with a large neck was playing soft jazz on a horn. Bobby slowly approached the casket, paused, and then stared into

Lester's face. He placed his hand on his friend's. "Thanks Lester, for all your help. I'll never forget you as long as I live."

Instinctively, he began singing "Old Man River". The horn player accompanied him. The mourners grew silent as they listened to his rendition. In the end, tears gushed down his cheeks. Everyone began chanting, "Alleluia, Alleluia." The horn player approached him and gratefully shook his hand. A few of the other mourners followed. Bobby just stood silently staring at Lester.

*　　*　　*

It was a dismal day. The cemetery was dark and dreary, and the wind was full of swirling debris. A black station wagon led a small procession through the narrow lanes of the lackluster memorial park with its rows of insignificant grave markers. The air was crisp. Overgrown foliage tangled in wild abandon.

The pallbearers solemnly carried the casket to the deep grave opening cordoned off by yellow emergency tape. Most of the mourners were from the musical community. They placed long-stemmed white chrysanthemums across his coffin and then walked away. Bobby was appalled at what he observed. The plywood-covered gravesite, and the cheap-looking casket, confirmed what Morgan had said—Lester had no money. At that moment, he wished that he had enough money to pay for a better funeral for his friend and mentor.

After the funeral, Morgan drove Bobby back to his apartment. He waved in a gesture of thanks as he disappeared into the building.

*　　*　　*

Mourning the loss of a relative or friend is never easy. Bobby felt depressed for several weeks. He just sat around, not even concerned about a job. In tribute to Lester, he practiced. His voice cracked at times, but the practice paid off. He noticed a vast improvement in the quality of his voice. Though his self-confidence grew, he knew that without professional experience it would be difficult to get an audition. A short stint at Morgan's place hardly qualified. If it weren't for the improvement in his voice, he would no doubt give up and go home. Bobby decided to stick it out as long as his funds held out. In the meantime, he still needed a job to eat and pay the rent, so he planned on pounding the bricks again in the morning.

Practice time again, Bobby thought. He stood in front of the bathroom mirror and practiced for more than hour. Later on, he scanned the help wanted ads in the newspaper, and wrote down the names and addresses of a few possibilities.

*   *   *

At the crack of dawn, Bobby washed, shaved, and put on his best suit. He stopped at a diner for a cup of coffee while he prepared his itinerary for the companies he planned to visit. His first stop was at a sweater manufacturer that required a stock clerk filling customers' orders. The eight-dollar an hour salary wasn't much, but he needed the money. He was told to report at eight the next morning for administrative processing. Although he was satisfied, Bobby decided to visit the other companies on his list in the hope of finding a better paying job. He was confronted with the same old story—better paying jobs required more experience. He threw the list in a trash container and continued hitting the bricks.

Suddenly, Sandy entered his mind. He decided to take a detour to Joey's place. As he sat at the bar with a drink in his hand, she was nowhere to be found. He turned to John the bartender. "Say, I don't see Sandy. Is she working today?"

John leaned over and whispered, "Sandy had a falling-out with the boss; something about her fooling around with another guy."

"What happened?"

"She quit and went back to Chicago."

That takes care of that, Bobby thought. Since it was early afternoon, he decided to visit the local library to search for a listing of agents. On his way, he passed a theater on 48th Street that was holding auditions for a chorus singer. The line of applicants was long, and he waited two hours to perform. As he scanned the theater, he saw the front row of judges. They appeared weary from listening all day. Bobby finally reached the end of the line when he was approached by the stage manager carrying a clipboard. He jotted down Bobby's name and then asked if he had any professional experience. Bobby could hardly explain that he had worked at Morgan's for the past few months, so he answered yes. But when the manager asked for references, Bobby's audition was cut short. The least

Bobby expected was a chance. He was wondering if his friends back home had put him on by telling him that he was ready for the big time. Bobby spent the last hour of the day at the library and then headed home.

* * *

He was crossing 43rd Street when he noticed a small sign fastened to a door—ARTY MANN AGENCY.

That's strange. How did I overlook this agency? I covered just about every inch of Manhattan Island. Hell, what do I have to lose?

A dingy stairway led him to the second floor. The frosted glass set in a dark wooden door repeated the name of the agency in large gold letters. Inside, the small office looked as though it was anything but a successful business.

Behind a desk to his right sat a very attractive woman with cascading red hair that looked as if it had been dyed. She was wearing a form-fitting blue mini dress, which revealed her long thin legs that she had crossed over each another.

"Can I help you?" she asked in a pleasant voice.

"Yes, my name is Bobby Shane. I'm a singer looking for an agent."

A door slowly creaked open, and out stepped a man smoking a cigar. He was about fifty, five-foot-six, overweight, and completely bald except for a few tufts of hair above his ears.

"A singer, Arty," the receptionist announced. "This is Mr. Bobby Shane. He's looking for an agent."

"Fine! Fine! Come in and sit! What's your name again?"

"Bobby. Bobby Shane."

"Pleasure. I'm Arty Mann. I'm a theatrical agent. Now, uh, tell me about yourself—like your experience."

Here we go again. He calmly explained himself, prepared to be refused.

"Fine." Mr. Mann interrupted him while looking down at his watch. "It's ten o'clock. Charlie Marx, my associate and piano accompanist, is due in around eleven. Take a coffee break on me. Stella will take you to the corner snack shop. Charlie should be here when you return."

* * *

"Just get in town, Mr. Shane?" Stella asked as they walked to the luncheonette.

"Bobby, please. No, I've been here for several months." He told her about his experiences finding an apartment and an agent, and singing at Morgan's Ale House. Most of all, he talked about Lester. They entered the luncheonette.

"Hi, Stella, what will it be today?"

"Good morning, Tommy. Tommy, this is Bobby Shane. He's a singer auditioning for a job with our agency. Tommy is a writer, and one day he will have a big hit right here on Broadway, right, Tommy?"

"Come now, Stella. You'll have him thinking I'm a Jerome Kern."

"Really? A show writer?"

"Sort of. I'm currently working on a musical. I should have it completed in a few months."

"Can I read it when you finish it?"

"Sure!" Tommy then excused himself and attended to the other customers.

"Have you known him long, Stella?"

"For the better part of two years. We're neighbors on the same block in the Village. He dropped out of college, left his hometown of Saginaw, Michigan, and ventured to New York to try his hand as a playwright or a show producer. 10:45—better get back. Charlie should be there about now."

Arty took him into the music room adjacent to his office.

"Bobby, I want you to meet Charlie Marx—the best piano accompanist this side of Chicago."

"Pleasure to meet you Bobby. What's your key?" His broad grin revealed gold-capped teeth, and his wire-rimmed glasses gleamed in the brass piano light. As his fingers glided over the keys, Bobby suddenly realized that he did not have his music arrangements with him and quickly decided on a song that he and Lester used often. Bobby sang slowly and softly, remembering Lester's coaching. From his piano seat, Charlie turned toward Arty, smiled, and winked.

After the audition, Arty and Charlie went into his office. From the waiting area, Bobby was only able to hear the murmur of their voices, so he moved toward the door to listen.

"I caught your wink, Charlie. Can I assume that he's good?"

"Not good Arty—great! This guy has the potential to be an exceptional singer. I'd sign him on quickly and get him started right now."

With Charlie's voucher, Arty fumbled in his desk drawer for a blank contract form. He grinned sheepishly as he rubbed the palms of his hands together. Charlie recognized the look; he'd seen it before. Arty was a very selfish person.

The door swung open.

"You have a superb voice, Mr. Shane. Here is what we have to offer you: you sign on with us as your agent and we'll keep you working."

"Great, I'm looking forward to starting."

"I get my usual twenty-five percent cut." Arty stared at Charlie, who was not surprised. He knew that Arty would cheat his mother out of her last dime. "One more thing—for recordings, if any, there is an additional percentage that we'll discuss if and when the time comes."

Bobby did not know much about the business part, nor how to rate the package. At the moment, he couldn't care less. He signed the contract and offered his hand. "Deal, Arty. I mean, Mr. Mann.

"That's okay Bobby. We're partners now. Let's keep it in the family. Call me Arty."

*　　*　　*

Arty called Bobby into his office and told him that he would be starting at The Pink Swan Club in two weeks. That would give him time to work with Charlie and to buy a new tuxedo.

"What do you have in the way of formal wear?"

"I have a tuxedo that's not too good. It's been cleaned and pressed."

"Okay, but another should do it. I'll advance you a few hundred dollars. You can reimburse me in a few small monthly payments. Pick up another tux, two shirts and a few ties. Plan on rehearsing your routine with Charlie before opening night."

"You got it, Arty."

"If I don't see you until then, I'll meet you there at six on opening night."

*　　*　　*

Arty convinced Stella to invite Bobby to her place for dinner. Initially, Stella hesitated. She felt awkward with the unusual request. A little coaxing and money from Arty for steaks convinced her to agree. It was Arty's idea to make him feel like a part of their little family.

Stella hurried to catch up to him. "Congratulations. Arty is interested in you."

"Thanks."

"Look, go to Bernard's for your tuxedo. It's just down the street. Meet me here at five-thirty and we'll go to my place for dinner. Later, I'll show you The Pink Swan if you want to know where it is."

"Your place for dinner? I won't be putting you out or anything?"

"Not at all," Stella assured him.

Bobby took Stella's advice and browsed through Bernard's Formal Wear display of various suits and accessories. He ordered a tuxedo, two shirts and a handful of ties. The tailor said he would have the alterations ready in one week.

Bobby looked down at his watch and saw he had time to walk around Times Square. He felt jovial and hoped this was the big break he'd been dreaming about since his childhood. He looked up at the marquees along 42nd Street and imagined his name on all of them. He suddenly thought of calling Mary with his good news.

"Operator, a collect call please to Mary Rich, Cincinnati, Ohio, number—"

"Mary? Hi! Bobby here. I have great news to tell you. I got a job with an agent. I'm starting in two weeks at a club called The Pink Swan."

Mary didn't try to interrupt him. Sensing his excitement, she allowed him to continue. When she had a chance to speak, she asked if he was eating properly and getting rest. Then he suggested she visit New York to see him perform.

"That would be nice. I'll check with Daddy, and maybe we can arrange a trip to New York."

"Have to go, Mary. I'll call you before opening night, okay?"

"All right, good luck. I love you."

*   *   *

At five-thirty five, Bobby hurried to meet Stella. Her old green Ford was parked in a lot on 43rd and 7th Avenue, so he knew she was home.

He walked around her apartment with his hands in his pockets. "Nice place you've got here Stella."

"Care to freshen up? The bathroom is the first door on the right. Extra towels are in the linen closet to your left."

He slid the medicine cabinet's door open and helped himself to deodorant, washed his face, and swished some tap water in his mouth.

The aroma of sizzling steaks filled the apartment and aroused his appetite. He watched her carry a tray with two mugs of coffee to the table. For the most part, they ate in silence, wondering about each other. Dinner was an extra treat for Bobby because it was his first home cooked meal since eating a farewell dinner with Mary's family.

"Great! Just great!" he said, patting his stomach. "Tell me Stella— was this your idea, or does Arty have you invite all his new clients to your apartment for dinner?"

Stella nearly choked on her food. 'The fact is, when you walked into the office today, I looked into your lonely brown eyes and you reminded me of a lost puppy."

He paused for a moment to reflect and then asked her, "You have anything like a steady boyfriend?"

"No, I'm strictly playing the field; for the time being anyway. I don't want to belong to anyone but myself for now."

His eyes locked with her eyes and she suddenly felt uneasy. "Well, I must do the dishes and clean up the kitchen. I'm the maid as well as the cook and dishwasher."

"Can I help?"

"No thanks. You know what they say about too many people in the kitchen. Just make yourself comfortable in the living room and I'll join you when I'm through." Her voice trailed off as she disappeared into the kitchen.

Bobby retreated to the living room, sat on the sofa in front of the television, and propped his feet up on a stool.

A few minutes later, Stella joined him. "Now that you are rested, tell me about yourself."

"There is not much to tell. I am an only child from a middle-class Cincinnati family. My parents died before I was twenty. I've lived on my own ever since, except for the Riches, who looked in on me once in a while. I enjoy singing, and I'm trying to make a living at it. The best I have been able to do so far is sing at local social gatherings. I had a job at a bank once, but my last job was as an accounting clerk for an advertising firm. Now, here I am. End of story."

"Girlfriends?" Stella asked.

"Sure. Zillions," he teased.

"No, seriously, anyone in particular? Like back home?"

"Not really, except for Mary. The Riches were my mother's best friends. Mary is their daughter. We have known one another since birth. We grew up together, Mary and I." He paused to think and then added, "Just neighbors, strictly platonic. Nothing beyond friendship."

"Sing me a song, Bobby?"

"Sure. I thought you would never ask. Would you like to hear anything in particular?"

"No. Just anything."

He sang his rendition of "Love Me".

"Wow! That was beautiful."

"Thanks for your enthusiasm. If everyone on opening night thinks like you do, I'll have no problem becoming a successful professional singer."

He leaned back and fell asleep. Stella made him comfortable with a pillow and a blanket, and then slipped his shoes off.

Bobby awoke to the sound of Stella showering. He lifted his body far enough to see the clock. It was six o'clock. He hadn't intended to stay the night. He stretched, rubbed his neck, and yawned. He used the kitchen sink to splash water on his face. *A shave would be a lot better*, he thought while scratching his beard.

She emerged from the bathroom wrapped in a Turkish spa robe and a towel around her wet hair. Her slippers scuffed along the floor. She let out a long satisfied sigh. "Your turn."

*   *   *

The typically heavy New York traffic made for a somewhat lengthy ride to The Pink Swan Club.

"Well, there it is, Bobby." From her seat behind the wheel, Stella pointed to a two-story brick building with pink and white trim. "Can you guess why it has pink and white gingerbread?" she laughed. "Well, it's cozy and clean; no rowdies. A step up from Morgan's Ale House."

As they neared his apartment building, he thanked her for the ride.

"My pleasure," she purred. "Any time."

Sure-footed and full of anticipation, he bounded up the steps to his apartment.

*   *   *

It was the final day of rehearsal. Bobby and Charlie had fine-tuned their part in the evening's program. Stella helped by serving them lunch. Occasionally, she caught him watching her. Her looks, mannerisms, and personality were a distraction. She loved every minute of it.

Charlie interrupted his trance. "You're not going to get it any better than that for now, though we still have to work on your timing and iron out a few wrinkles." But Bobby wasn't satisfied—he practiced every night.

CHAPTER 2

The billboard read "Welcome to The Pink Swan" in large pink and white letters. Just below, in smaller lettering: "Featuring newcomer Bobby Shane". Anxious, he had arrived at the club early and was greeted by Mr. Gordon, the owner. Being early would afford him the time to familiarize himself with the club. As he wandered about, he found himself in the center of the stage. The anticipation brought a lump to his throat. He was confident this would be the start of his professional career.

Band members began filing in carrying their instruments. Arty and Charlie were close behind. "Hi ya, Bobby! Did you just get here?" asked Arty.

"No, I've been here forty minutes or so."

"Good."

Charlie introduced him to the band members, then they sat at a side table to discuss the evening's performance. Charlie had a dry run with the band and the headliner, and then Bobby sang two songs.

It was almost show time. Bobby stood in front of a mirror and nervously adjusted his tie. He looked handsome in his black tuxedo, cummerbund and bow tie. His ruffled shirt made him feel smart.

*   *   *

"Introducing the dashing and debonair singing sensation from Cincinnati, making his debut at The Pink Swan—let us give a warm welcome to Bobby Shane!"

Charlie led the band with "A Lovely Day". That was Bobby's cue to make his way on stage. He reached the microphone and began singing. His next song was "Lonely Hearts"; despite his nervousness, he sang it perfectly. Gordon turned to Arty. "I have to hand it to you, Arty. You may have found yourself a diamond in the rough. With a bit more experience and polish, I think he has great potential."

When Bobby finished his fifth number, he bowed and looked over at Stella, who was standing and applauding heartily. His next song was the finale. Bobby took his bows and left the stage for his dressing room.

"Well Charlie, what do you think? How did I do?"

"Good. Very good."

"Thanks, Charlie."

Arty walked in, clapping his hands and smiling. "Gordon liked you, Bobby!"

Arty grabbed a champagne bottle from the cooler, popped the cork, and began to pour. He raised his glass. "Here's to the newest number one singer to hit New York!"

Bobby felt as giddy as a kid in a toy store.

After the second show, he mingled with the audience. Many extended their congratulations, and a few offered him a drink to toast his successful opening. Elated, he thanked them and continued to make his way around the club.

At closing time, Charlie teased him. "Going to sleep here tonight, Bob?"

"Oh, hi, Charlie. It was a very exciting opening for me tonight, but I'm feeling a bit tired."

"I know how you feel," Charlie said. "I'll drive you home."

*   *   *

Though the rest of the week went well for Bobby, people weren't knocking down his door either. But Bobby was smart enough to know that he had time on his side. And he knew that those who attended his shows left satisfied. Most important of all, he was working.

*   *   *

Bobby's payday at The Pink Swan made him very happy, even though he received less money than he had expected. "Hey Stella, look—I'm rich!" He waved the check above his head.

"Tell you what—ask your boss for the afternoon off. We'll go to my place. I'll take care of some bills and then we'll go out on the town to celebrate my good fortune."

Stella looked at Arty, who nodded his approval. "Let's go before he changes his mind." She took Bobby by the hand and they exited the club.

"Here," she said as she tossed him her car keys. "You drive."

"Thanks, Stella. You're all heart. I don't know if I can handle this New York traffic yet. Besides, my driver's license expired."

"No excuses. You're driving."

"Okay, you asked for it."

Bobby had trouble clearing 43rd Street. He slammed on the brakes and brought the car to a screeching halt at the first red light. When the light turned green, he stepped on the accelerator and sped through the intersection. The wheels squealed as he turned a corner. With her eyes closed and teeth clenched she braced herself for a potential collision, but he had kept a sharp eye out for other vehicles.

When the car was safely parked and the engine turned off, she looked at him wide-eyed, "Whew! I think I made a bad decision telling you to drive!"

*   *   *

His repeated knocks failed to get a response from Slade. "Hell, he's not in, Stella. Let's go up to my room and I'll check again on our way out. It's my turn to make you a drink, okay?"

"Fine. Wow, you need an elevator," she remarked while climbing the stairs.

"No elevator. You just need to get in shape."

"Oh yeah? Well, I see you're puffing a little, too."

He opened the door and stepped aside for her to enter first. She could feel his breath against her face when she passed in front of him.

"This is it?" she asked sarcastically.

"What do you expect for seven hundred dollars a week—the Taj Mahal?"

"No, but at least hot and cold running water," she said facetiously.

"Funny, Stella—it just so happens that I have hot *and* cold running water."

Without warning, he pinned her against the wall and kissed her cheeks and neck. She pressed her hands against his chest. "Wait. Where's that drink you promised me?"

He ignored her and continued kissing her face and her neck. Then they moved to the bed. Their moans of passion reverberated through the thin walls of his apartment.

In a few moments, there was a loud rapping on the door. "Hello? Is anyone in there?"

"Slade! Could he hear us from the first floor?" Bobby hurriedly dressed himself.

He opened the door and greeted his landlord. "It's okay, Mr. Slade. It's only me and a friend."

"Ok, Mr. Shane. For a moment I thought there were burglars in here. By the way—your rent is due for this month."

Bobby paid him his money and began to close the door. Slade held the door for a moment, focusing his eyes on Stella before returning to Bobby. "Remember what I said about no girls after dark."

"Sure, sure," Bobby said impatiently as he shut the door.

"Persistent cuss, isn't he?" she laughed.

"He's okay. A little strange, but harmless. Tell you what—make yourself at home while I freshen up. We'll do the town and celebrate."

"Sounds good to me." She sunk down in a soft chair and waited while he cleaned up.

Once they were outside, she tossed him her car keys. "You did such a good job getting us here, you deserve another chance."

"Don't press your luck."

"There's a great steak house in the Village, not far from where I live. Let's try it, okay?"

"Sure, why not?

The restaurant lacked the ambience of a good steak house, but the aromas were inviting. He was pleased that the steaks tasted as good as they smelled. Poets, singers, and other artists provided free entertainment. They were much like Bobby, just not as lucky. They were still waiting to be discovered.

*   *   *

Bobby successfully completed his stint at the Pink Swan. He was satisfied with his performance, but he felt that there was more to learn. Remembering Lester's instruction, he practiced his breathing exercises and stomach control at least an hour a day.

*　　*　　*

Arty wanted to make certain that Bobby kept on working. The next available gig was a weekend engagement at the Stardust Ballroom. Bobby would be the featured vocalist, and Arty pointed out that he needed the exposure.

His Friday night performance was well-received. On Saturday night, a huge crowd of twenty-five- to sixty-year-olds were in attendance. A few who were supposed to be ballroom dancing stood in front of the stage just listening to Bobby sing.

*　　*　　*

Bobby performed at various cabarets in downtown Manhattan. Most of the clubs were small and intimate, like Morgan's place. But his exposure was slowly bringing him more acclaim. Arty was able to book Bobby at an upscale supper club. Bobby was excited that the patrons listened and paid attention when he sang. Arty also booked him for a few one night gigs in the Village. The money wasn't the greatest, but it would help him move up the ladder of success.

*　　*　　*

Following Charlie's advice, Arty gave Bobby a week off to work on a new routine. It was just as well, since Bobby had nothing booked for the next week. During this time, Charlie sensed that Bobby's voice was beginning to peak. Bobby continued practicing and even started recording their rehearsal sessions. It took only three days to complete their new routine. For the next two days, Bobby sat with his tape recorder. He played it over and over again, listening for any flaws that needed to be corrected or adjustments that needed to be made.

*　　*　　*

Bobby's name was becoming well-known in the local entertainment scene. He was given a one week engagement at Atlantic City's Club Tiki—just in time for the summer vacationers. He also started making more money. The club was nearly filled to capacity the first night. Bobby was happy to have the time to spend his mornings sunbathing on the beach and relaxing in the afternoon. Stella was able to visit him for a day or two before heading back to the city.

*   *   *

Arty was offered a return engagement at the Pink Swan with an increase of money, which he immediately accepted. Mr. Gordon had been following Bobby's progress. He wanted him to perform at his club before Bobby became a star and would command much more money for his performances.

*   *   *

Stella's apartment building finally had a vacancy. After months of being on the waiting list, Bobby rented it immediately. With her help, he furnished himself an attractive bachelor's pad. When their decorating was finished, he admired what they had done. "I have to admit it, you are finally right for a change."

"Wow, listen to you. Give me an hour to fix supper. We'll celebrate your new place."

At Stella's apartment, Bobby enjoyed himself so much he lost track of the time. He glanced at the red numbers of the digital clock across the room. "Wow, look at the time! I have to get going!"

He slung his coat over his shoulder, and then left for the club. With only a few minutes to spare, he saw patrons lined up to enter an already jammed nightspot.

Mr. Gordon was the first person he met on his way backstage. "Hello, Bobby. Did you see that crowd out there?"

"Yes, I noticed. Who's coming, the President of the United States?"

"You! They want to see Bobby Shane."

After the show, Arty was anxiously awaiting Bobby in his dressing room.

"Good news, Bobby. Mr. Charles Hartman is going to be in the front row during the second show. He wants to watch your performance."

Bobby looked at Charlie and then back to Arty, "Who is Charles Hartman?"

"He's only the owner of The Top Hat Night Club on Broadway, that's all. Playing his club is a stepping stone to the big leagues and bigger bucks," Arty said.

Charlie concurred. "He's on the level. This could be the thing we're all looking for. Go out there and knock 'em dead."

During the comedy act, Bobby stood at the bar, scanning the audience. Although he had never seen him before, it was easy to pick Mr. Hartman out of the crowd. He was a suave-looking, dark-haired, three-piece—a stern businessman who studied the program's schedule and checked his watch every five minutes.

Bobby took a final sip of his drink and went backstage to prepare for his performance. He made his entrance to the tune of "Dark Secrets". Thirty minutes later, he ended with "Something to Remember", and then bowed to a rousing ovation. One of those clapping the heartiest was Mr. Hartman.

Bobby paused to straighten his hair with the palm of his hands and adjust his tie before entering Mr. Gordon's office. Hartman was there waiting for him.

"You have a fine voice, Mr. Shane. I'd like to offer you a two-week engagement at my club, with a guaranteed salary of fifty thousand dollars."

Stunned by the amount, Bobby could barely get one word out. "Agreed."

Mr. Hartman turned to Arty for approval. "Mr. Mann?"

"Yes, sir. Yes, sir. Fine, sir. Just fine." He was just as nervous as Bobby.

With everyone in agreement, Hartman sent for his lawyer to draw up a contract. "Mr. Finch will fill you in on the details. See you in two weeks."

Gordon's office came alive. He broke open a bottle of champagne and they all toasted to Bobby's success.

Bobby finished his drink in one swallow. "I want you to work with me, Charlie. I sure can use you, especially now."

"You talked me into it." Charlie smiled and pompously puffed out his chest. "We'll start a new routine right away."

During the next week, Bobby and Charlie rehearsed their new routine—morning, noon, and night.

*   *   *

Bobby decided to check out The Top Hat Nightclub. He hailed a cab to drive him downtown. As he entered the cab, Lester crossed his mind. He directed Mike, the cab driver, to take a detour past the cemetery, and to stop at a floral shop along the way.

Bobby knelt and placed the floral arrangement at the head of Lester's grave. His eyes noticed the grave marker. It was made from salvaged wood.

"I told you that I would never forget you, Lester. You deserve the credit for my success." Tears welled in his eyes.

CHAPTER 3

The Top Hat was one of New York's finest nightclubs. Bobby walked around the back and noticed the rear door had been left open. He peeked in and saw workers cleaning the floors and polishing the brass railings. No one challenged him, so he toured the club. He was awed at the elaborate décor of rich woodwork, oriental carpets, and gigantic crystal chandeliers. A bar made of mirrors and glass framed one side of the room.

*   *   *

Saturday arrived, and Bobby's fans filled The Pink Swan to its capacity, knowing it was to be his last performance at the club. His finale commanded a standing ovation and he gave them four encores. The audience was delighted yet sad to see him go.

A group of his fans greeted him in his dressing room, where they threw him a small farewell party and wished him continued success.

The club bouncer, a burly bodybuilder, whispered in Bobby's ear, "There's a young lady in the entrance who insists she's a friend of yours. Her name is Mary Rich."

Without a word, Bobby rushed darted toward the foyer.

"What was that all about?" Arty asked.

"I don't know. I told him was somebody asking for him out front.

As Arty rushed to catch up with him, he saw Bobby embrace a young woman.

"Oh, Bobby, it's so good to see you. I missed you so much, but I feel better now that I see you."

Bobby took her hand and led her to his dressing room. "Everyone—I want you to meet a very special friend of mine. This is Mary Rich."

Mary blushed and smiled. "How do you do?" she said politely as she sat on a folding chair. His fans acknowledged her and then returned to their partying.

"Sit and let me look at you. How long have you been here? Where are you staying?"

"Wait, one question at a time." She laughed as she grasped his hand. "Daddy came to New York on business and he brought mother and me along because he knew that you were here in New York."

"That's great! Where are they now?"

"Daddy had to return to the hotel and meet with business associates. He'll come for me when I call him."

"Nonsense, I'll take you. Call your father and tell him that you're with me and that I'll see that you get back safely." Bobby gave her the phone, and then approached Stella about borrowing her car.

After Bobby thanked everyone in the room, he left with Mary.

*   *   *

Bobby's fingers tightened around the steering wheel as he negotiated the busy New York streets. The clubs were letting out, causing traffic jams. He passed his first apartment building, Gilliam's garage, and Morgan's Ale House. He told Mary about Lester as he drove across town to his apartment.

"What do you think?" he asked.

"Nice. Very nice!"

"Have a seat and I'll get you something to drink. Soda pop is all I have, okay?"

"That's okay it looks like you lost a few pounds. Are you on a diet?"

"No, it's all the running around I've been doing."

"Yes, apparently. Mary stared at the doorjamb intently.

"What's wrong, Mary?" Bobby took her hand and held it to his chest.

Mary avoided looking toward him. "Would it mean anything to you—?" Her voice trailed off; then she flipped her hair and glared resentfully at him. "If I said I missed you, would that mean something to you?"

"Oh, hey, Mary. Sure, I'd—you, you've always been my special—I'd never do anything to hurt you. I—"

"I'm like the sister," she said flatly, pulling her hand from him.

"Well, we've had some great times together, you and me. But right now, I'm up to my ears in this thing and I've got to get it together."

"Your dream?"

"Right, right. When I feel like I'm getting there, then I can get on with my life." Bobby saw tears in her eyes.

"Well, that's it, then. I should be getting back."

"Look, Mary, let's talk about this after we've both had a chance to think. You've caught me off guard. How 'bout tomorrow night? I'll—"

"Daddy has something planned." She pulled her jacket around her and fluffed the collar. "Mother and I are quite important in his life right now."

Bobby felt the sting of her words long after she had left. *Jerk*, he thought to himself. *Are you as stupid about women as you appear?*

* * *

Mary went back to her hotel room, fell across the bed and sobbed. Her mother heard her cries through the adjoining door.

"Oh, mother, what am I to do? I love Bobby so much, but he doesn't love me except as a sister."

Her mother tried to console her. "Of course he loves you, dear. He just doesn't know it, yet. You must understand that he is working to become a professional singer. That's demanding work. And, it's his dream, honey. He has to give it a chance. He'll always wonder if he could have made it. I have a feeling that once he makes it, he will settle down. Give him time."

"Do you honestly think so, mother?"

"Yes, I do."

* * *

After the final show at The Pink Swan, Arty gave Bobby two days to rest. Two days were all he needed. He was rejuvenated and eager to start his new assignment. Mary and her parents had returned to Cincinnati.

*   *   *

The Top Hat was brimming with excitement. The Bobby Shane Fan Club had followed him to his new venue. There were a few show business insiders in attendance, at the invitation of Mr. Hartman. He had invited them to critique the performance and to help predict his success.

Bobby didn't appear to be nervous as he slowly sauntered into the spotlight, but his stomach was churning. What if he lost his voice? What if the critics gave him a negative review? He would let down his promoters and himself. Arty had said that playing at The Top Hat would be "a stepping stone to the big leagues and big bucks." He took a deep breath and thought of Lester's advice. "Don't let the audience dictate to you. You dictate to the audience."

He acknowledged the crowd's applause with a slight bow and then performed his opening number. By the fourth song, the audience had begun to warm up to him. When Bobby finished his repertoire, he left the stage with his fans on their feet.

He returned to the stage and performed an encore of medleys. The patrons demanded more. He raised his arms gesturing for silence. Eventually, he was able to speak.

"Thank you, thank you all very much. You're a great audience, and I would gladly sing for you all night; however, there's a second show later tonight, so there is more coming."

His second show was as successful as the first. Bobby Shane's first evening at The Top Hat was a success.

*   *   *

Stella, Charlie and Bobby spent the night at Arty's apartment. "We'll have a quick breakfast and wait for the first editions to hit the street," Arty announced. "Then we'll find out how well Bobby did."

Arty and Stella anxiously waited for Charlie to return with the reviews. Bobby was still sleeping. When Charlie bounced in with three different newspapers, Bobby Arty and Stella each grabbed one. The room buzzed as they each tried to read aloud at the same time.

Arty called for quiet. "Hold it down! Not so loud. Jerry Walker of The Times says, 'Can't miss Shane: biggest singing sensation since *Sinatra*'."

"Listen to this one," Stella added. "'He could sing for me anytime'— Shirley Johnson, The Gazette."

Bobby commanded a turn. "I got the best one—listen to this. 'In addition to being a great singer, Bobby Shane has just enough ham in him to make it as an actor. I predict that he is going to make the big time."

"Who wrote that one?" Arty asked, stretching his neck for a closer look.

"Let's see—oh, yes—Charlie Scott, The Mirror."

"Hey, great! His word means a lot in this business."

*   *   *

Bobby felt fantastic. He was among the big names now and had purchased his first status symbol—his own automobile. He wouldn't be borrowing Stella's anymore. He'd gotten a used Black Lincoln with plenty of extras. He took it for a test drive along the East River with Stella beside him.

"Lots of luck, sweetie. It's a beauty."

"Thanks, Stella. You can borrow it when you need it."

"Oh? Thanks a lot," she said with a chuckle.

It was a beautiful day for a leisurely jaunt along the River Drive, and he drove its entire length. The bright sunlight bounced off the windows of cars ahead of them. The radio was playing soft, relaxing music. Stella sat back and enjoyed the ride.

Between the comfortable ride and the soft music, they lost track of the time.

"Wow, 7:45!" he exclaimed, looking at the car's digital clock. "I have to get ready for tonight. Hang on, Stella; you're in for a ride!" He pressed the accelerator and spun the car around.

*   *   *

Lester's memory lingered in Bobby's mind. In his mind he saw Lester at the piano, his thin fingers against the white keys, his foot pressing down on the pedals. *Thanks again Lester. You deserve credit for my success.*

Later that evening, Bobby told Stella that he was running an errand in the morning and wanted her to accompany him.

"Please telephone me at nine. That's when I want to wake up."

"Sure, Bobby. Whatever you say."

He didn't need her to wake him. He had been unable to sleep.

His errand took him along East River.

"Where are we going?" Stella asked,

"East side."

"East side? What's there?"

"A funeral home. Let's see—I'm looking for 163rd Street," he said, stretching his neck to read the street signs. "Ah, here we are—Anderson's funeral home."

As he had pulled against the curb to park, she wondered who had died. By now she had met all of his local friends and didn't recall anyone passing away. "Are we attending a funeral?"

"No, you'll see."

Mr. Anderson answered the knock on his door.

"Hi, Mr. Anderson," Bobby said as they entered the funeral home. "I don't know if you remember me but-"

"Sure. You're Bobby Shane, the singer who is appearing at The Top Hat nightclub. You were Lester Brown's friend from Morgan's Ale House."

"That's right, Mr. Anderson—you have a good memory."

Stella sat quietly and listened to the two men discuss a memorial for Lester at Bobby's expense. "Something special for him," he explained. He wanted an exhumation and reburial in a better part of the cemetery with the largest gravestone they would allow. Mr. Anderson made all the necessary arrangements.

*   *   *

Lester's former pastor presided over the proceedings on a rain-soaked day. Strong winds and bolts of lightning hadn't kept the forty mourners away. Those that couldn't fit under the tent watched the proceedings from under their umbrellas.

After the service, everyone shook Bobby's hand as they passed by. They left through the cemetery's narrow winding roadways for the luncheon. Bobby remained at the grave a little bit longer. "Good-bye, Lester. I told you that I would never forget you. I feel you're keeping a close watch over me. Sometimes I sense your presence. You will always be in my heart."

*   *   *

Bobby was awakened by a knock on his door.

"Bobby, it's Stella."

"Hi Stell, what's up?"

"It's Arty. He'd like to speak with you, and he's waiting in my apartment."

"Arty? Here?" *Something's not right*, he thought. "Why would he come here to the village just to see me?"

"I don't have the foggiest. But he's here." They proceeded to Stella's apartment. Bobby opened the door slowly.

"Hello, Arty. Out of your territory, aren't you?" he kidded.

"Hi, Bobby. No, I'd go to the end of the world to see you." Arty appeared nervous. He paused, looked around the apartment and then continued, "You know Bobby, I was thinking. Since you're working in Manhattan, I kind of figured, jeez, why should Bobby travel from the Village to Manhattan, possibly getting stuck in traffic on the way to the club."

"Hell, I don't mind Arty. I have a car now, and Stella for company. I allow myself plenty of time to get to the club. These arrangements are just fine."

"Wait, Bobby. Arty may have a point."

"Okay Arty, what do you think?"

"I'm thinking maybe the Manhattan Towers."

"The Manhattan Towers?" Bobby looked over to Stella in shock.

"You're talking money, Arty. Big money. which I don't have at the present time."

"I know that. That's why I'll carry the load for a few months."

"I don't know Arty; let me sleep on it. I ll let you know later today, okay?"

"Okay, Bobby. See ya, Stella."

"For the second time in two weeks, I smell something fishy. How about it, Stell?"

"He's a hard man to figure, Bobby. It's obvious that he wants you close by. My guess is that he wants to make certain that you get to the club on time. It is a beautiful hotel, though. I say take it since he's picking up the tab. If he's up to something, you'll find out soon enough. It wouldn't be wise to turn down anything that Arty's offers free."

*   *   *

Bobby called Arty that afternoon to tell him that he accepted his offer. With Stella's help, it took Bobby one hour to pack his belongings and travel to his new home.

While taking a nap in his room, Bobby was awakened by the telephone.

"Sorry to disturb you Mr. Shane, but there is a young lady here to see you. Says her name is Stella."

"Send her up—she works for my agent."

"Yes sir."

"Say, it's easier getting to see the President of the United States."

"Sorry, Stell. That's the price for being a celebrity."

"Oh wow, I'm standing next to royalty."

"Okay, okay, wise guy." Bobby tossed a pillow at her legs and threw her off balance. Her legs went high into the air as she landed on her buttocks. Bobby got a full view of her thighs. She noticed him looking and knew that it meant trouble.

"Forget it—I have to get back to work. I have a message for you, and you'll never guess in a million years."

"What's that?"

"Well-" She paused for a moment. "You've been offered a recording contract!"

"A what? Repeat that again, Stell."

"Records. Recording. You know—like in music."

"Well, I'll be a son of a bitch. That explains the reason for the hotel, picking up the tab—the whole nine yards." Bobby was more overcome by shock than happiness.

"Ah-ha," Stella laughed. "In fact, Mr. Ritter from Mecca Records is waiting for you in Arty's office this very minute."

After Bobby put on a clean shirt and tie, they headed for Arty's office. Arty was there at the door to greet him.

"Mr. Shane, meet Mr. Ritter of Mecca Records."

"Pleasure, Mr. Ritter."

"All right gentlemen, shall we get started?" Arty rubbed the palms of his hands.

"Fine, Mr. Mann. I am prepared to offer you a one-year contract for one hundred thousand dollars, plus royalties. We expect Mr. Shane to record a minimum of one album and five single records."

"No problem, Mr. Ritter. Is that okay with you, Bobby?" Arty grinned from ear to ear.

"Absolutely!"

"Very well, gentlemen. I will have the papers drawn up in the morning. Can you start this Monday, Mr. Shane?"

"You got it, Mr. Ritter. Monday morning it is."

Bobby watched Mr. Ritter as he disappeared down the stairs. Then he turned to Arty. "You're a sly old bastard, Arty. You knew about the recording contract when you offered to finance my move to the hotel, didn't you?"

"Sure. And I would have made the same offer even if this didn't happen. You have to admit, it's closer to the club for you."

"I know, Arty. You are taking good care of me." Bobby wrapped his arm around Arty's shoulder. "Only no more surprises, ok?"

"Sure, Bobby. Understood."

Bobby walked toward Stella, who was giggling. "Go get em, tiger," she whispered to him.

*   *   *

Bobby, Arty, and Charlie arrived at the main gate of the Mecca Record Company. A security guard greeted them. "Yes sir, can I help you?"

"Yes—Mr. Shane reporting for his recording session'."

"Mr. Shane?" The guard perused his list. "Ah, Mr. Shane! Straight ahead one block, brown building. Report to Mr. Steel's office."

Mr. Steel greeted them and welcomed them to Mecca Records. "Mr. Ritter sends his regards," he announced. He went on to explain that there would be two to three days of preparation, consisting of song selection, music arrangements, and rehearsals with the band. The final step would be recording in the studio.

Mr. Steel escorted them to the recording studio and introduced Bobby and Charlie to Mike Manning, the bandleader. Charlie and the band went over the music arrangements while Bobby selected the songs for the recording. With all in agreement, they began rehearsing. The entire session went smoothly. Bobby and Charlie were told to return the next day at ten o'clock.

The recordings were completed in seven days. Mr. Steel was pleased with the results. Then they reported to Mr. Ritter's office.

"I want to thank you all for your work. Bobby, I hope this is the beginning of a long relationship with Mecca Records."

"Thank you, Mr. Ritter. When will the recordings be released?"

"Figuring in promotion and distribution of the records, I'd say two to three months."

*   *   *

Arty accepted a one week commitment at Ciro's, a posh hotspot in the city. It boasted an elaborate exterior façade. Inside, polished brass railings guided guests to their tables. The dark wood décor and oriental carpets made Bobby realize his dream was becoming reality.

"When do we open?" Bobby asked.

"Three weeks from Saturday," Arty answered.

"Does Mr. Hartman know?"

"No. I'll tell him after the first show tonight."

With the first show completed, Bobby and Arty went to Hartman's office to inform him of the gig at Ciro's. Hartman was surprised, but happy for Bobby, and he congratulated him. "And you too, Arty; you're doing all the right things for Bobby."

"Thanks, Mr. Hartman."

"Tell you what, Arty. Since Bobby doesn't open for three weeks, how about holding him over here for two more weeks? That still gives him a week off for rest and preparation."

They all agreed on the proposal.

In a happy frame of mind, Arty turned to Bobby and said, "The way things are going, we have a shot at playing Vegas soon."

"How soon?" Bobby asked.

"There's a rumor around town that Las Vegas executives are coming East in about three or four weeks. It's part of an annual search for new talent. Al Hunt, the entertainment editor for The News, will keep me apprised. I'll let you know when I get the word. So what do you think?"

"You're doing a great job."

*   *   *

Tickets for opening night at Ciro's had been sold out since flyers were first distributed, announcing his performance. Word had reached Arty that Las Vegas scouts were in town, incognito. Their mission was to look for singers who could be ready to move to Vegas on short notice. Bobby was in that category, but Arty was unable to find out if they would be at any of his performances. Nobody knew, not even Al Hunt.

On Saturday night in Ciro's packed lounge, Bobby shared a booth with Arty in a reserved area.

"A ballpark figure, Arty. How much do I have in my account?"

Arty scratched his chin, wondering what was on Bobby's mind. "Um, off the top of my head, I'd say about twenty g's or so.

"That's great!" He picked up the phone and paged Stella, who was sitting at the bar. "I'm on my way to my dressing room—meet me there."

A few moments later, Stella came through the door. "Hi, sweetie. What's up?"

"As a token of my appreciation for you taking care of me these past few months, I want to buy you a fur coat. Charge it to Arty's account, since I don't have an account of my own yet. And Stella, don't spare the expense."

"You don't have to do this sweetie—you treat me just fine." Her eyes sparkled as she leaned forward and kissed his cheek.

"I know I don't have to do this, Stella, but—" He pointed his finger at her. "You're buying the coat." He smiled and added, "It's cold in New York."

*　　*　　*

As he lay in bed gazing up at the ceiling, Bobby thought about Mary. He reached for the phone to call her. Mrs. Rich answered.

"Bobby, we are so very proud of you. You're always in the paper, and folks are talking about getting a group together and seeing your show."

"Thanks. That's great, Mrs. Rich. I, ah—"

"You want to speak to Mary?"

"Yes, please."

"I'm sorry, but she stayed back in New York, looking for work. Maybe you can talk her out of it—we couldn't."

"She has a phone?"

"I don't have the number yet—can you believe it? She said she'd call. But I'm so glad to hear from you."

"If she phones, I'll track her down."

"Oh, if you would. Let me have your number, and I'll tell her to get in touch. This is just not like her—she needs a scolding."

CHAPTER 4

After the first show, Bobby hurried to his dressing room. Arty, Stella, and Charlie were waiting for him, each wearing I-know-what-you-don't-know grins.

"What's happening?" he asked.

The talent spotters had liked his crowd-pleasing performance and raced to grab the budding artist. Arty had dollar signs dancing in his head. He walked across the room toward Bobby clapping his hands. He shook Bobby's hand vigorously. "Never a doubt, Bobby. You caught the eye of the Vegas scouts, and now they want Bobby Shane. I can take care of the particulars. Same contracts as before, okay?"

"Absolutely." Bobby then paused for a moment while he reconsidered his answer. "No, not okay." It was his opportunity to demand more money. He had been getting anxious about Arty's financial interest for a while. "Your commission percentage gives me heartburn."

"What's that, Bobby?" Startled, Arty arched his back.

Bobby placed his arm around Arty's shoulder. "You have chutzpah, but I'm catching on to you. We need to renegotiate."

Arty broke into a sweat. For the first time, agent and singer were at odds. Their eyes locked, their egos clashed. "Don't forget your dream to be a Las Vegas entertainer," he said, pointing his finger at Bobby. "Without me, you would be nothing more than a saloon singer."

This time, the tactic didn't work. Bobby looked long and hard at Arty. "I wonder how all the other agents are surviving with only ten to fifteen percent commission."

"Okay. When we finish this tour, we'll renegotiate. How's that?"

"No. If you want to continue being my agent, I want your commission reduced to fifteen percent, now!"

"Wow, don't you trust me."

"No."

"Oh, hell." Arty moaned as he rewrote a new agreement. Bobby signed the papers and Charlie signed as a witness.

Then Arty broke open a bottle of champagne to seal the deal.

* * *

Arty made the necessary arrangements for the two-week engagement at the MGM Grand. His salary was raised to a hefty fifty thousand weekly. He wanted Stella to go with him.

"I want you to come with me. You're my good luck charm."

"I know how you must feel, but I can't. I'm sorry, sweetie. Arty told me that I have to stay here to keep the agency going."

"Okay, I don't want to interfere with Arty's business. But promise me that you will fly out the first chance you get."

"I will, I promise."

"Good! Now I need a favor."

"Sure, sweetie. What is it?"

"Do you remember Mary Rich? She's the girl from my hometown."

"You mean Mary who showed up at the club's cocktail party?"

"Mary didn't go home with her parents. She stayed in New York to find a job. Since I won't have time to find her, see if you can track her down for me. I promised her mother I'd look for her. Hire a private detective if you have to. She was staying at the Midtown Hotel the last I knew. I told her this is no place for her. I just want to find her to say good-bye and try to talk her into going home. By the way, did you shop for the fur coat?"

"No, but I'll do both, first thing in the morning."

* * *

Stella had left for the Fifth Avenue furrier at nine o'clock, dressed in a dark blue hooded sweatshirt and blue jeans. A sales woman followed her around the high-class store. With anticipation, Stella browsed the racks of designer coats. It gave her the feeling of rubbing elbows with the wealthy. But she felt awkward spending Bobby's money. Finally, she had selected the one she wanted: a lush three-quarter length male silver fox. She was so thrilled, she dreamed of wearing it the entire day. Then her daydreaming was interrupted by the task of finding Mary. She charged the coat to Arty's account, then hurried out.

Stella called Bobby several hours later. "I found her!"

"That's great! Where?"

"The Endress Hotel."

"How did you find her so fast?"

"Oh, I have connections."

"Thanks again—I really appreciate it."

*　　*　　*

At the Endress Hotel, Bobby asked the building's concierge for Mary's room number.

"She requested no visitors," the concierge replied.

Flashing a twenty-dollar bill persuaded the clerk to relax the rules. He snatched the money and obliged him. "Room 2121. Use the elevator on the left; it's an express."

Bobby knocked persistently. "Mary, it's me, Bobby. Please let me in. I have to talk to you." His plea rekindled a romantic fantasy in her. She opened the door, sunk into a nearby chair and looked down at her folded hands. She wondered why he was there.

"Mary, you're not thinking wisely. Do you think it's easy to get a job in New York? Besides, there are criminals roaming the city. You may not be safe here by yourself."

"You're just a friend, Bobby, not my father. Did my parents ask you to come here?"

"No, your parents didn't ask me to come here; and I know I'm not your father. I'm your friend. This is what friends are for."

He soon realized he was not getting anywhere. "All right, have it your way. I came to tell you that I'll be leaving New York for Las Vegas at the end of this tour. I'm scheduled for two weeks at the MGM Grand,

and I hoped you would be as excited about it as I am. It's been my dream and now it's happening. I would like it if you called me."

She was upset when he said he was leaving New York. Her jaw dropped, her eyes widened. She drew in a deep breath and gave out a long sigh.

* * *

Closing night at Ciro's was sensational—tickets for the last show had sold out quickly. Bobby performed five encores before the crowd allowed him to leave the stage.

* * *

Arty had his apartment decorated as though it were New Year's Eve. A local print shop had made a BOBBY SHANE MEETS LAS VEGAS good luck banner. When Bobby saw Stella, he relaxed and warmed to the event. They danced the night away. Intoxicated, he spent the night in Arty's spare room. It was noon when they awoke.

"Okay, Bobby, up and at 'em. We have a plane to catch, unless you want to use your broom."

"What happened?" He lifted himself on his elbows. "My head—it's pounding and feels swollen."

"Inebriated. You were inebriated," Arty answered as he handed him a glass of his homemade hangover remedy.

"Phew. What is this nasty tasting concoction?"

"It's a secret recipe."

It worked in no time. Bobby called Stella to say good-bye and remind her that he wanted her in Las Vegas and soon as possible.

"I'm practically on my way," she quipped.

CHAPTER 5

The casino-lined main street of Las Vegas offered plenty of entertainment. Bobby and Arty sun bathed on swimming pool lounge chairs while enjoying the scantily clothed girls.

"This is the life, Arty. I may just retire here for an entire year. No more New York winter weather."

"You deserve it. Enjoy it—it's all yours for a while. No work; just the sun, women, fresh air, and more women."

*　　*　　*

The evening before the premier, Bobby indulged in a little gambling in the hotel's casino. Arty joined him later at the craps table.

"Be careful, Bobby. This could get in your blood."

"No problem, Arty. I'm only investing a few bucks."

Thirty minutes later and still holding his own, he eyed a tall, gorgeous blonde at the blackjack table.

"Over there, Arty. Look!"

"Bobby, if you're looking at what I call ice cubes, take some advice and quit drooling."

"I'd like to wake up next to that every morning."

"Yeah? And I once read about a guy sleeping with his pet python."

"How the hell do you know? Don't be steering me off. Are you my mother now?"

"She's a circuit rider. I met her at a party a year ago. She's known. She has a taste for luxury and loves to gamble—and I mean big time." Bobby took a long swallow of the bourbon and ginger. "Name?"

"Norma Stone. But forget it. I don't even know if she'd remember me."

They both walked over to where she was seated.

"Ah, Miss Stone—Arty Mann here. I believe we met at the Farnsworth's a year ago."

"Oh, yes, Mr. Mann. You're an agent, right?" she said, batting her eyelashes.

"Right. May I present my client, Bobby Shane? He's the vocalist opening here tomorrow night."

"Of course. Your reputation precedes you, Mr. Shane."

"Thanks," he said, shaking her hand.

"Would you like a drink, Miss Stone?"

"No thank you, I'm about to leave. I have an early appointment." She looked at her fingernails as if to suggest the appointment was with a manicurist.

"Okay. How about dinner tomorrow night?" he asked.

Sorry, Mr. Shane. I'm busy tomorrow night." Sensing his disappointment, she continued, "I generally have breakfast at pool-side. Usually at eleven."

"Great! It's a date?"

"Yes," she chuckled. "See you then."

She left the casino, deliberately swaying her hips as she put one foot in front of the other. Bobby watched her until she disappeared.

"Man oh man!"

"I told you, she's cold as ice. A real snob."

He hadn't heard a word. "Isn't she something?"

"Don't let yourself get carried away. She's dangerous."

"I appreciate your concern, but I think I can take care of myself. Thanks for the warning anyway."

*   *   *

Bobby anxiously awaited Norma at poolside as the morning neared eleven o'clock. He wondered if she'd come at all. When he spotted her, his heart swelled. She was delicious looking.

"Good morning, Miss Stone."

"Good morning, Bobby."

During their breakfast, he couldn't take his eyes off of her sumptuous body. She wore a short Turkish towel robe over a white bikini. Her blonde hair was gently blowing in the morning breeze.

After breakfast, she excused herself to keep an appointment.

"When can I see you again?"

"Really can't say. I'm staying in room 212. Give me a ring."

For a whole week, he tried unsuccessfully to reach the elusive Norma.

*   *   *

Bobby and Charlie had arrived long before show time. It was Bobby's opening night at the MGM Grand. They met the band and coordinated the details with the bandleader. With all the arrangements made, they retired to Bobby's dressing room to await curtain call.

Bobby walked on stage to a standing ovation and performed so well that he ended the show with five encores.

The entire two-week engagement went flawlessly; he performed to a capacity crowd every night.

After the final performance, the management wanted to extend his contract. In spite of an offer to increase his salary, he declined. Bobby wanted to go back to New York.

*   *   *

Though he was happy to be back in New York, Bobby wasn't in the mood to go to his apartment alone, so he went to Stella's for a rendezvous. He just put his bags down when they hugged one another. They spent a romantic night together.

He had slept until the telephone woke him up. Stella handed him the receiver. It was Arty telling him to be in his office by eleven o'clock to meet with television representatives.

"Okay, I'll be there."

*   *   *

A throng of people filled Arty's office: agents, lawyers, television and corporate executives, and a few prominent journalists. Reporters photographed Bobby signing contracts for two California television talk show appearances and a two-week singing engagement at a luxurious Las Vegas casino hotel.

In the background was Mr. Hartman, owner of The Top Hat nightclub. He was moving toward Bobby with outstretched hands. "Congratulations on your success, Bobby."

"How are things at the club, Mr. Hartman?"

"Holding my own."

"What brings you to Arty's office?"

"I need a singer to fill in for a week."

Bobby turned to Arty. "Book me at The Top Hat for next week."

Surprised, Mr. Hartman glanced over at Arty and quickly back at Bobby. "I appreciate it, but I'm afraid that I can't afford to pay you what you're worth."

"No problem. I'll do it on the same terms as before."

Same terms as before! Arty thought to himself

*   *   *

Bobby, Arty, and Charlie were sitting in The Top Hat's lobby when they spotted Norma gliding across the room, her beautiful long legs in full stride.

"Hello," she said softly.

The three men rose to their feet to greet the woman who was fast becoming the object of Bobby's attention.

"Hello yourself," Bobby shot back casually.

He excused himself from the group and took her aside. "What are you doing in New York? I had tried calling you in Las Vegas."

"I'm sorry. I rushed to my mother—she needed me."

"Do you have dinner plans tonight?"

"Come to think of it, I don't."

"The last show doesn't start for another three hours, and I haven't eaten yet. I would be flattered if you would have dinner with me."

"That would be nice. Yes, I'd love to."

The restaurant they decided on boasted of authentic, made-to-order European cuisine. Marble statues lined mahogany paneled walls. The high ceiling was complemented by long maroon velvet drapes. A dark-suited maitre d' seated them at a table for two with provincial style chairs.

The dimly lit room was accented with white tablecloths, linen napkins, fresh red roses in a crystal vase, and glowing candles. Soothing violin music played in the background.

Bobby couldn't keep his eyes off of her. Norma's beauty and poise mesmerized him. They touched glasses and she gave a toast, "To your success, Bobby."

She had already sized him up. She wanted him. He had the means to provide her with the lifestyle she sought. If she poured on the charisma, he would be thinking she was made for him.

After dinner, they strolled to a quiet out-of-the-way alcove in the hotel lobby. Bobby watched her as she sat in the over-stuffed chair, leg over leg. In his imagination, he was making love to her.

A familiar voice brought him back to reality. "Almost show time, Bobby. Better get going!"

*   *   *

After the show, Bobby, Arty, and Charlie were sitting at a round lounge table chatting about the latest events. As they spoke, someone entered the room.

"Hi, Mr. Mann." It was Tommy Simms from the 42d Street luncheonette.

"Tommy Simms! How are you? Care to join us for a drink?" Arty asked.

"No, thank you, Mr. Mann."

"What's up, Tommy?"

He looked at Bobby and Charlie with reservation.

"Speak up, boy. No need to be timid. You're among friends," Arty continued.

He pulled a chair over to the table and speaking directly to Arty. "Well, Mr. Mann, I just completed writing the musical I told you about a year or so ago, and I'm looking for a partner to help finance its production."

A sinking feeling came over Arty. Surely, Tommy would be asking for money. "Oh, boy," he muttered. "I should have known. How much do you need?"

"Two hundred thousand dollars. It has the makings of a great show, Mr. Mann. I know it."

"How do you know it? Are you a critic or something? No, I'm sorry. I just can't do it."

"The writer," Bobby said. He sat straight up and addressed Tommy. "I remember you. You're Tommy, from the luncheonette. Am I right?"

"Yes sir, Mr. Shane. The 42nd Street luncheonette."

"Sure, sure. I was with Stella."

Bobby rested his chin on the back of his hand as he thought. "Mmmm. Two hundred thousand dollars."

"Wait Bobby," Arty said. "Think it over before you invest."

He ignored Arty and looked at Tommy, "You really believe this show will be a hit?"

"I can taste it."

"When would this musical open?"

"Approximately six to nine months—maybe sooner."

"What would be my percentage of the take?"

"Fifty percent."

"Whoa—fifty percent? When can I see, uh, what do you call the show papers?"

"Libretto," Tommy answered. "I have a copy in my car."

"Bring it to me. I would like to see it."

Bobby soaked in his drink while scanning the pages. He acted as if he knew the value of what he was reading. "Mmmm, seems pretty interesting."

He took his checkbook from his coat pocket. "Whom to, Tommy?"

"Me."

"Good luck, Tommy," he said as he handed him the check. "Keep me informed of the progress."

"Thank you very much Mr. Shane. You won't be sorry—I promise."

"Oy vey. Listen to the clairvoyant," Arty mumbled. "Boy, when I need money, I'll know where to go."

"You already know where to go," Bobby said pointedly. Then he picked up his drink and went to his dressing room to relax.

*　　*　　*

His final night at the Top Hat, Bobby played six encores before leaving the stage. After the show, he prepared for his trip to Las Vegas and California. Stella made his traveling arrangements and drove him to the airport.

*　　*　　*

Upon his arrival at the Desert Inn Hotel, Bobby was escorted to the Penthouse suite.

During his first show of the evening, Norma waltzed in and sat at a small table near the stage. Her presence was palpable to the other patrons as soon as she entered the room. The edge of the white spotlight highlighted the gold in her blonde hair and her jewelry sparkled as the light passed through their prisms.

Bobby took the microphone from the stand and moved slowly through the audience toward her as he sang. During the applause, he leaned toward her and whispered, "Stay until I'm finished."

He read her sensuous red lips he longed to kiss. "Yes," she answered.

After his final song, he didn't acknowledge the curtain calls. He was anxious to see Norma.

"I'm having dinner brought to my suite. Care to join me?"

"I'd love to," she purred.

She walked ahead of him into his room and entered that world of luxury she longed to be in. To be a part of it, she needed to seduce the handsome and available Bobby Shane.

After the meal, they lounged on the sofa. Bobby pulled her closer. Their lips met for a long, hard kiss. She stiffened when he reached for her breast. She relaxed and allowed him the liberty, but only for a moment. She then withdrew and asked for a drink. Having regained his composure, he poured her a glass of Grand Marnier.

Norma was smart enough to nurse the cordial, knowing that it was almost time for Bobby's next show. He perceived Norma's tactic, stood up, and grinned. "Have to go; it's show time." He kissed her cheek and returned to his dressing room.

*   *   *

Bobby completed the second show with six encores. Instead of going to his dressing room, he and Charlie went to the bar for a drink. Arty was already there sipping club soda. Arty informed Bobby that he'd been receiving many phone calls with big offers for Bobby's services. Bobby smiled and told Arty to go for it.

"I want all the money that I'm able to earn."

Arty was all smiles. "You got it, Bobby."

*   *   *

"Yes, who's there?" Bobby answered the intercom.

"The First Lady of the United States. Who do you think?"

"Stella?" He dashed to the elevator door, took her in his arms, and kissed her.

"Sit. How about a drink?"

"Yes, gin and orange juice."

"How long are you going to be here?"

"Three days."

"Does Arty know that you're here?"

"Not the foggiest."

They had agreed that she would share Bobby's suite during her short stay.

He passed through the lobby on his way to meet Charlie, and found Arty reading the Wall Street Journal. The paper crinkled as he folded the page down to get a better look at Bobby's happy face. It was obvious that Stella had the remedy to relax Bobby's tension.

"My, aren't we feeling chipper? Should I guess?"

Bobby flashed his toothy grin. "You couldn't guess in a million years."

"Wanna bet?"

"Save your money, Arty. This one's on me. Stella is upstairs! She's in my suite!"

"Stella? My Stella?"

"No, *our* Stella, Arty."

"You're right. I never would have guessed."

In his happy state of mind, Bobby performed exquisitely. He gave three encores before leaving the stage.

*   *   *

The three days passed quickly and Stella had to leave. On the way back to the airport, he handed her a box wrapped in blue silk.

"Our friendship is special, and I want you to have this."

Overwhelmed at his generosity, she nervously opened it to find a diamond necklace. Radiant with joy, she reached over, hugged him. "Thank you."

*   *   *

Norma had been bragging about Bobby to her friend Irma.

"He's so handsome, Norma," Irma said, looking at his picture. "I can see why you're chasing after him."

"Not to mention loads of money, darling," she said with a sly grin. "Loads of money."

"Do you think that you can get him?"

"My darling Irma—he is at the breaking point now."

*   *   *

Arty was anxiously awaiting Bobby's return from the airport. Bobby laughed at the sight of Arty hurrying through the main entrance toward him.

"Easy, Arty. What's your hurry?"

"Do you think I've been waiting here to amuse you? Go ahead and laugh. You have an hour to catch a plane to California."

Bobby's eyebrows came together as he wrinkled his forehead

"What?"

"You're scheduled for a talk show tomorrow night, and you have a three-night gig at a Beverly Hills hotel."

"Yeah?"

"Tickets are at the terminal, our bags are packed, and a car will be here in a few minutes. So turn around."

*   *   *

Bobby, Arty, and Charlie walked out of the Los Angeles Airport into the sun-drenched afternoon after their short flight. A stretch limousine was waiting to transport them to the studio of a late night show, the first stop in his circuit of talk show appearances. The folks at the studio were all smiles and handshakes.

The influential hostess began the brief interview.

"Are you married?"

"No, I'm single and on the prowl," Bobby chuckled.

"I hear you are working on an album."

"Yes, I've recorded four songs so far."

Norma had been tuned in and listened to the interview with great interest. She quickly arranged a trip to California.

*   *   *

Bobby, Arty, and Charlie met for dinner at the Beverly Hills hotel.

"Hey Bobby, look over there," Charlie said, nodding toward the entrance. "It's that what's-her-name?"

"Norma Stone," Bobby answered.

She confidently approached the table. "Hello. Aren't we far from home? What brings you to California, Bobby?"

"I'm starring here this week."

"That's great. I'll make certain to catch your show."

Bobby stood up. "Would you care to join us for a bite to eat, Norma?"

"I'd love to."

Bobby pushed a chair back and seated her. Soon after, Arty and Charley wisely excused themselves.

Bobby invited her to take in the sights of Los Angeles.

"Great idea," she answered. They planned the next day's itinerary, finished eating, and each went there separate ways. Norma couldn't stop smiling.

*   *   *

Bobby and Norma spent the entire day riding taxis in and around the city. They had brunch at the posh Brown Derby restaurant. They toured the MGM studios. They returned to the hotel and shared intimate moments. It wasn't what he had hoped for, but it was a step in the right direction.

*   *   *

Bobby and Norma were now an item. They were seen together dining in Beverly Hills. They made the gossip columns in every major newspaper and on television entertainment shows. Arty was disappointed. He now knew that the advice he given Bobby in Vegas was all for naught. He had hoped that Norma would change her gold-digging ways by being straight with Bobby and truly loving him.

*   *   *

Mary was too busy with her work to notice the attention surrounding Bobby and Norma. But her mother noticed. She phoned Mary to complain about Bobby's behavior.

"Mother, it's Bobby's business what he does." Mary pretended that she didn't care. "If that's what he wants it so be it." She cut her mother short and hung the phone. Deep in her heart, she hoped that Bobby was just infatuated with Norma.

* * *

Bobby's tour in California was extended. He continued to perform to sold out crowds, and Norma attended every performance. It was only a matter of time that Norma would get her man.

* * *

The hectic schedule was beginning to take its toll on Bobby. Arty realized that it was time for his client to rest. Bobby agreed to take a few weeks off. He spent the next week at the hotel, sleeping late into the mornings and lounging poolside in the afternoons. In the evenings, he took in the shows in the hotel lounge. Norma was by now almost always by his side. As he sat by the pool, he thought about proposing. He thought about Mary and how she would react. But he knew he wanted Norma. That evening, while he and Norma were in the lounge, he proposed to her.

"I thought you would never ask," she sighed happily.

* * *

It came as no surprise to Bobby's friends when they heard him and Norma announce their engagement. Even though Stella was disappointed when she got the news, she had expected it would happen. She had made it quite clear from the beginning—no strings.

* * *

Mary had sat quietly at her kitchen table, drinking her morning coffee and reading the newspaper. She saw the wedding announcement in the gossip column of the entertainment section and gasped. The more she stared at the words, the more she became distressed. She didn't take the news well. She began to shake. Angry, she fought to hold back her envy. The paper crackled as she rumpled it and threw it into the trash container. "Hope you'll be happy, Bobby."

*　　*　　*

A silver Rolls Royce limousine waited for the bride and groom to emerge from the ceremony. In front of their many family and friends they had promised to love, honor and cherish one another forever.

Behind the barricades, hordes of fans waited for a glimpse of the newlyweds. The wedding was as big an event as expected, filled with celebrities, gossip columnists, and the paparazzi. Bobby looked regal in his charcoal gray tails and polished shoes, but it was Norma who got the public's interest. Dressed in a shimmering white beaded gown and wearing a diamond-studded tiara, she looked as though she stepped out of a wedding magazine.

"What's wrong, Bobby? You look pale," Arty teased.

"Nah, just a little nervous. This is my first time." He struggled with a smile. He thought the procession of well-wishers would never end when he saw Stella next in line.

"Stella, what can I say?"

"Not a thing, sweetie. Just be happy. This seems to be the best thing for you."

"Stella, you're the best friend I could ask for. Don't forget, anything I can do for you, you got it."

"Sure sweetie," she sniffed. A tear rolled down her face as he kissed her wet cheek. "I always cry at weddings."

*　　*　　*

From his bed, Bobby patiently watched the doorway, waiting for his bride of just a few hours. Seeing her enter the bedroom, he felt euphoric. *Just beautiful*, he thought as he studied her from head to toe. She wore a semi-sheer white negligee that revealed her long slender legs. She was a masterpiece. She came closer and closer until everything she owned became visible. Pulling her close, he wrapped his arms around her body. He wanted to explore every inch of her. Her mind was on the life of luxury she had entered. She had married Bobby Shane. Both experienced a night of passion.

*　　*　　*

A week later, Bobby cursed when the phone rang. He wanted to sleep a little longer. As he blinked his eyes, he grabbed the phone from its cradle.

"Yeah, who is it? What do you want?" he grunted.

"It's me, Arty."

"Don't you know what time it is? Call me back later, Arty."

"Never mind the time; I have good news for you. I'll be right up."

Before Bobby could say another word, Arty had hung up.

"It's Arty, Norma. He says he has something very important to tell me."

He hoped it wouldn't be news about the press or interview possibilities, or talk show appearances. He was weary of show business talk and backstage gossip. And money—always money. After a few moments, Arty entered their room.

"Okay, Arty. What's so important that you had to wake me this early?"

"Hi ya, Bobby." Arty wore a huge smile and rubbed his palms together. "Hollywood. In two weeks! You have an appointment in two weeks for screen tests."

Bobby just stared at him. His heart began to race and then slowed down when he thought it was a joke.

"Arty, it's too early in the morning for jokes."

Norma wore a big smile, yelping and jumping up and down with joy. Like Arty, the dollar signs were dancing in her head.

"On the level. I wouldn't joke about something like this!"

When he realized Arty wasn't teasing, Bobby became ecstatic. "Hey, that's great! Sit and have a cup of coffee with us. I'm not totally awake."

While they sat drinking Arty brought Bobby up to date explaining everything in detail. Thrilled by the news Norma prepared a batch of bacon and eggs to which they would celebrate. Arty excused himself and left.

*   *   *

One week later, Arty contacted Bobby. "You have a date with International Studios on the fifteenth for your screen test. I'll fly over two days earlier to lay the groundwork for a deal. I won't know until then when I will be able to negotiate a contract. As of now, you will be making one motion picture. Because it's your first venture in films, we'll probably accept whatever they offer."

"Thanks, I know that you'll get me the best deal."
"See you later, Bobby."

*   *   *

Arty and Charlie took a four o'clock flight to California. Arty had made arrangements for Bobby and Norma to follow two days later.

"You're all set. I have your plane tickets and a hotel reservation. I'll leave them at the front desk. Charlie is going with me; you and Norma are to follow on Friday. I'll check with you Thursday night to make certain there's no change."

"Okay, Arty, I'll be waiting for your call. Thanks."

*   *   *

Norma declined to go along. "I'm staying here at least another week or so. You will probably be too busy and I would only be in the way. I may join you later."

*   *   *

To play the devoted wife, she went to the airport to see him off. There were the usual Bobby Shane fans and the paparazzi. For show, he gave her a peck on the cheek. After a final wave to the crowd, he entered the ramp leading to the plane and took off for Hollywood.

*   *   *

Arty was waiting at the airport to greet Bobby and Norma.

"Norma isn't with me. She decided to wait a while before coming out."

"Okay, let's go to the hotel and get settled."

CHAPTER 6

Bobby's preconception of Hollywood was confirmed by the hustle and bustle at International Studios. He and Arty were introduced to the studio head, Mr. R. J. Sinclair. Sinclair was a tall man with piercing dark brown eyes and a crop of black hair flecked with gray that bounced when he walked.

Bobby had his picture taken with Sinclair and some of the studio's actors and crew before a brief walk-about. He was given a tour of a cavernous building with smaller studios along the perimeter. One room held the props, another was a sitcom studio for a current television show. Each of the studios was numbered, and each studio had its own sound room.

A luncheon was given in his honor after the tour. The conference room was abuzz with staff wanting pictures and autographs.

Arty left him with Marvin Cox, director of photography, who introduced him to the men behind the cameras. Cox led him to his studio on the opposite side of the building.

Marvin's studio wasn't very large. It had a blue screen that draped on to the floor. Several photo lamps, two silver umbrellas, and a reflector board on wheels, stored against a wall, surrounded it. A large portrait camera was pointed at the backdrop from its tripod perch. Bobby was in awe of the entire complex of equipment.

"With all this equipment, I can see why your photographs are so good, Marvin."

"Equipment doesn't make a photographer good," he explained as he turned on the high-powered lamps. "It's the photographer's eye in capturing the subject. What the person is wearing is important. It portrays his mood. The film's speed and lens filters are important, too. Stand over there." He pointed to the middle of the blue rug.

"Today we'll be photographing you from many angles. This way we'll know your best side and see how you take to the camera. Any questions?"

"No."

"Good, let's begin."

Bobby was instructed to strike a variety of poses, and was photographed from nearly every conceivable angle. Cox noticed Bobby becoming tired, so he called an end to the shoot.

"That's it for today, Mr. Shane. We'll complete the final portion in the morning."

Bobby wondered how a model could pretend to laugh or cry when he or she was not in the mood.

*　　*　　*

The next morning, a limousine arrived at the hotel at seven-fifteen to shuttle him to his first screen test.

At the studio he was greeted by Mr. Cox. "Good morning, Mr. Shane. Did you sleep well?"

"Great. I really enjoy waking up with the birds."

"Well, you know what they say."

"Never mind what they say."

"As you look around the studio, you will notice that we are using more sophisticated cameras and equipment today."

"I notice," Bobby answered, impressed with what he saw.

"We'll pick up where we left off yesterday—same routine."

There were four cameras set up to capture Bobby's movements. The lighting was basically the same, but with colored filters. A general director and a technical director were in a dark room behind the scenes sitting in front of four monitors, one monitor per camera, controlling the equipment.

"Any questions, Mr. Shane?"

"No."

"Good, let's begin."

Marvin viewed him from behind one of the cameras. Bobby could hear the filters snap into place, and the camera motors made a whirring sound as they moved. The lights gave off a lot of heat, and before long, Bobby started to feel the strain. His muscles were beginning to tire when a voice came through a sound system. "Take a break now," Marvin said. "Take thirty-five minutes, please."

After the lunch break, it was time for the screen test. In the sound studio he met Ken Johnson, a man of short stature with thinning black wavy hair and dark brown eyes. Bobby was given a script to read and then instructed to act it out while the cameras rolled.

* * *

He met Arty in Sinclair's office where they were gathered to discuss Bobby's ratings. Yes, he was photogenic. Yes, he passed the screen tests. He had been considered; now he was accepted. It was time to discuss a contract. Bobby agreed to one motion picture and a percentage of the gross profit. If the film did well, there could be a sequel.

With all in agreement, Sinclair ordered the contracts drawn up by the legal department.

"We start shooting in two weeks. We'll begin work on the soundtrack right away."

* * *

Being alone gave Norma the freedom to drink. She had successfully hid her dependence from Bobby; now she was making up for lost time. She also gambled heavily. After a day-long shopping spree, Norma and Irma sat beside the pool. Irma was envious of her friend, but happy for her at the same time.

She was aware of Norma's drinking and gambling habits, and thought that it was time for her to be responsible in her marriage.

"Slow down, Norma," she urged.

But Norma wouldn't hear of it. "My darling husband is making money hand over fist. He should spend it on *me*. I'm his wife—I deserve it."

* * *

The tall, well-groomed maitre d' who handed him a telephone interrupted Bobby's meal. "Mr. Shane, you have a long distance call from Las Vegas."

"Quido here, Mr. Shane. I'm the head cashier at the casino. I have a marker signed by Mrs. Shane for twenty thousand dollars. I must have that amount by Friday."

"Twenty thousand? You must be kidding me. It can't be that high!"

"I wish I was sir. But I have to have the money by Friday."

"Thanks, Quido. I'll have the money sent to you quickly. Oh and listen, Quido—she is cut off as of now, understood?"

"Yes sir. As of this minute."

Bobby shook his head and looked up at the ceiling. *What's happening?*

"Norma?" Arty asked.

"Better get her here, Bobby; as soon as possible."

"Don't worry, she'll be here. You heard me cut her off."

Arty wasn't the least surprised—he knew what Norma was capable of. But he didn't think that it would happen this soon.

Norma arrived as Bobby predicted, but she didn't show any anger. She asked Bobby for his love and he obliged.

*   *   *

The recording sessions for the movie soundtrack went smoothly. A meeting was held in Sinclair's largest conference room. Sinclair chaired the meeting from the head of the table. He introduced Jim Price, producer; and Ron Jordan, general director.

Then he turned the meeting over to Jim.

"It's a pleasure to be working with you fine actors and actresses again, and especially with you, my dear," he said, acknowledging the Swedish-born Sheila Ross, the film's leading lady. Sheila nodded graciously and then glanced across the table at Bobby. She had stared at him throughout the meeting, an act which distracted him immensely. When Jim Price called for a break, coffee and sweet rolls were brought in on silver trays and placed on a serving table.

Bobby poured coffee for himself and Arty, picked up a few sweet rolls, and returned to their designated area.

"How're you holding up, Bobby?"

"Not too bad, Arty. But I wish Miss Ross would stop staring at me."

"I think she goes for you."

"I bet she does."

He returned her stare, giving her the once over. He looked at her up and down and thought to himself, *not bad.* She was twenty-three years old and stood five-foot seven inches, with long jet-black hair and smooth milky white skin.

"Well, Mr. Shane, if Mohammed won't come to the mountain, the mountain must go to Mohammed," Sheila said as she presented her hand to him.

"Miss Ross, this is my agent, Arty Mann. I've seen your motion pictures Miss Ross, and I must say, you were great in all of them."

"I'm honored, Mr. Shane. It's not every day that I get a compliment from a great singer."

Bobby smiled at her graceful acceptance of his compliment.

"We will probably be seeing a lot of each other since we have the leading roles."

"Great."

The meeting commenced, and Jim gave his opening remarks. "Miss Jennings will be distributing your final scripts. We will meet here for the next three days, beginning at nine in the morning. That's nine sharp. We will go over the scripts and answer all questions. Now then, I'll turn the meeting over to Ron, who will be directing the movie."

"Thank you Jim; and good morning, ladies and gentlemen. I would like to begin by introducing everyone. Most of us know one another, but we have a newcomer among us—Mr. Bobby Shane. I hope that you are enjoying your stay with us and will continue to do so throughout the making of the movie."

Bobby acknowledged him with a nod and a smile.

Ron had explained how he expected everyone's full cooperation—that tardiness would not be tolerated. He then asked Miss Ross to help Bobby understand the signal system he would use during filming.

"This motion picture is about a singer, as you may have already predicted. Bobby Shane is our leading man; his character is Bobby Dell. Bobby Dell is a very successful singer; however, during the height of his career, he turns to alcohol to bolster his confidence. That not being enough, he then turns to drugs and becomes addicted. All this is noticed by his agent, John Forbes. That's you, Jim; you are Bobby's agent. John realizes that this is affecting his performance. John cancels his tour for a month to straighten himself out. Everything fails. Bobby is then forced to a rehab center and is introduced to Dr. Ann Dillman. That's Sheila. You take Bobby under your wing and love comes into play. Bobby, you will have the most difficult job—playing the part of an alcoholic and a drug addict. If you need help on how to portray both, we will have experts within the studio who can assist you firsthand knowledge."

Everyone laughed; Bobby smiled and nodded. Ron called for a break in the meeting.

"Mohammed is coming to the mountain this time, Miss Ross. It was a pleasure meeting you."

"Thank you, Bobby. I'm having some friends over to my house for dinner tonight. Care to join us? We could have dinner and then go over our scripts afterwards."

"It would be my pleasure."

"My chauffeur will pick you up at seven o'clock. Dinner is served at eight."

"Seven is good. Would you mind if I bring someone with me?"

"Not at all Bobby. I think that would be appropriate."

"Thank you," he said as he shook her hand.

*   *   *

Bobby stopped at the hotel's front desk to check for messages. The clerk found a note in his mailbox. "Ah, yes, there is something there." Bobby read the note: "I decided to do some shopping. Will be a little late. Be a dear and have dinner without me. Kisses. Norma."

He chuckled to himself as he folded the paper and put it in his pocket. *Perfect*, he thought.

*   *   *

The chauffeur arrived precisely at seven and brought Bobby to the party. Sheila greeted him at the door and looked surprised to find him alone.

"Oh, I'm sorry; my wife sends her regrets."

She took his arm and introduced him to the room. Her guests were from the entertainment business, drinking cocktails and nibbling on hors d'oeuvres.

"To be honest, I'm famished," she whispered.

"Ditto," he answered as he picked up a cocktail from a servant's tray. During dinner, each course was more fantastic than the one before it.

"Norma would have loved it," he thought to himself.

*　　*　　*

Sheila clapped her hands for attention. She told her guests that she and Bobby were going to the study to go over their scripts, leaving them in the care of her butler, Jason.

In the study, she pulled her chair close to his, then she crossed her legs and rested her script on her knee. It took Bobby's best effort to concentrate on the task at hand.

"Did you have a chance to browse your script?" she asked.

"No, not really. By the time I got back to my hotel and freshened up, it was almost seven."

"Your personnel script is prepared especially for you. What I mean is, that it's marked to make it easier for you to follow your lines. The one I have is a general script. Understand?"

"I think so."

"Good. Turn to page, um, let's see,—page twenty-two. The second line. Watch me." She acted the part to give him an idea of how it should go. He was impressed. When she finished, she pointed to a line she wanted him to try.

He read the line, and then looked up at her for approval. She paused.

"Pretty bad, huh?"

"To the contrary, Bobby—it wasn't bad at all."

They practiced their lines late into the evening. She was a good mentor, and Bobby gained a new appreciation of her talent. She was surprised at how quickly he learned.

"Tired?" she asked. "It's late—let's call it a night. We can meet and do this again."

"Sounds good to me."

"The car is ready, Miss Ross."

"Very good, Jason. Mr. Shane will be ready in a few minutes."

He took her hand in his. "Thanks, Sheila. You've been a gracious host."

"My pleasure."

CHAPTER 7

"Where have you been? Arty's been calling you for hours," Norma shouted from the dressing table.

Too tired to argue, Bobby explained that he had returned to the studio after reading her note.

"I wanted to do some studying and completely lost track of time."

"Well, don't make it a habit," Norma shouted back.

Bobby grit his teeth and headed for the shower. Even with the water running he could still hear her chastisements.

*   *   *

The next day's session went well. The entire cast stopped what they were doing as they watched Bobby portray an out-of-control drunk. By three o'clock, Bobby felt he had made good progress. Ron announced his pleasure at being ahead of schedule. He congratulated Bobby for learning his role so quickly and thoroughly. Bobby thanked him and swelled with pride as Sheila gave him an approving wink.

"Everything is going smoothly. I'm calling it a day. Tomorrow, instead of working on the scripts, report to wardrobe."

Norma wasn't happy to hear he would be working through dinner.

"I'll find something better to do," she pouted, and hung up.

Sheila overhead his conversation and sensed a problem. "Something wrong, Bobby?"

"Huh? Nothing, nothing at all."

"We could have dinner at my place and study there, if you would like."

"No thanks. I'd rather stay here."

Being the professional that she was, Sheila handled the situation superbly. She picked the scenes most likely to give them problems—in particular, the love scenes.

"Too tense. Much too tense. Try to relax. Now try again."

He took her in his arms and stared into her eyes long enough to generate real passion. His heart was pounding. He slowly pressed his lips against hers. Short kisses followed by long, hard kisses. He enjoyed every minute of it. He eased back and set her free.

She responded by gasping and patting her chest, "Wow."

"I can't wait to see what happens when you have this scene down pat."

"I feel guilty making love to a beautiful woman," he laughed.

"That's the price of fame."

As they walked out of the studio together, they agreed to continue their reading the next evening. Her car was waiting for her.

"Can I drop you off somewhere?"

"No thanks. I'd rather walk."

*   *   *

Bobby walked through the cocktail lounge of the hotel and saw a crowd at one section of the bar. Norma was the center of attraction, talking and laughing with three men. They quickly moved away when they saw him approaching.

"Oh dear, they deserted me," Norma said as her arms circled his neck and she kissed his cheek.

"My, aren't we popular tonight?" She was beautiful. He didn't blame them.

"Did you have dinner?" he asked.

"Yes, how about you?"

"I had dinner at the studio."

"And homework with your leading lady? What's her name?"

"Sheila Ross."

"Is Sheila beautiful?" Her lips puckered in a pout.

"Not as beautiful as you are, Norma."

He reached out to touch her cheek with the back of his hand. She'd obviously had too much to drink.

"How about taking a walk with me?"

"Okay." She took his arm and wobbled to the elevator.

How mysterious she could be. One day, cold as ice. The next day, warm and enthusiastic.

* * *

Bobby reported to the studio early, looking better than he had in a long time.

"Good morning, Bobby. You look well this morning."

"I feel great, Sheila," he said with a lift in his voice.

"That's what a good night sleep will do for you," she said with a wink and a smile.

"Yes, it's amazing, isn't it?"

The wardrobe fittings took four hours. They spent the afternoon with Ron, preparing for the first day's shoot. They rehearsed their marks as the crew tested the lighting and set up the cameras.

* * *

In New York City, Arty's new office included a large mahogany desk that rested in front of a wide picture window overlooking the New York skyline. Behind it sat a leather-padded high back chair. For fifteen minutes, Arty did nothing but test it—back, down, and around.

Stella laughed. Although she missed Bobby, she had little time to think about him since she'd started dating the realtor who leased Arty his new office.

Stella eventually married the realtor, with Arty acting as the best man.

CHAPTER 8

It was Bobby's turn to be filmed. He arrived at the studio early, anxious to get started. Henri, a make-up artist with a thick French accent was also ready. He led Bobby to the makeup room, sat him in a chair, and began applying makeup. Henri worked like an artist painting a mural. A dab here, a dab there. A little of this, and a little of that. With each application, he backed away and surveyed his work. It had to be perfect. Bobby was amused as he sat there watching Henri's every move.

"Fini, Mr. Shane."

On his way back to the studio, he passed Sheila's makeup room.

"Good morning, Miss Ross," he yelled in the door, which drew a complaint from Helga.

"Good morning yourself, Mr. Shane."

In her Swedish accent, she exclaimed, "Out, out, whoever you are! You are interrupting my schedule."

Sheila turned to her and spoke. "Helga, don't you know whom you're speaking to?" She laughed and winked at Bobby.

"Whoosh! I don't care if he's the Queen of England."

Bobby laughed and shook his head. He went directly to the wardrobe department to be outfitted for the role. Then he went to the set, where he found Ron and Sheila discussing the day's shooting script.

People on the set watched Bobby portray a drug addict suffering through withdrawals. Bobby's confidence as an actor increased with each compliment he received.

During the lunch break, Bobby, Sheila, and Ron rode to the commissary in Ron's golf cart. He congratulated Bobby on his fine performance.

"Don't congratulate me, Ron—congratulate Sheila. She's my tutor."

"Oh, Bobby." She waved her hand at him and blushed at the compliment.

*   *   *

The afternoon's shooting had included Bobby, Sheila, and a few cast members. Ron called it a day. "That's a wrap for today. Everyone be on the set at seven in the morning."

Bobby and Sheila left together.

"You were just great today, Bobby. If all goes well, we'll finish the picture on schedule. Maybe even sooner."

"Thanks to you, Sheila. I must admit that I'm really enjoying myself."

By the time they reached her car, Bobby had accepted her offer to drive him wherever he wanted to go.

*   *   *

After he checked for his messages, Bobby went to the lounge to look for Norma. He was happy she wasn't there, but surprised she wasn't in the room, either. A note on the night table read, "Bobby, darling: I'm spending a day or two with Irma in Las Vegas. Hope all is going well with your motion picture. Love, Norma."

Bobby grinned, crushed the note in his hand and tossed it in the waste container. He slouched down in a chair to read the next day's script but was interrupted by the phone. It was Mr. James, head cashier at the casino.

"Mr. James calling, Mr. Shane. The missus, sir—she's asking for a marker for an additional ten thousand dollars."

Bobby didn't want to spoil the good mood she had been in the past few days. "Okay, go ahead. Give her whatever she wants."

"Thank you, sir. And have a pleasant evening."

*   *   *

Henri had applied Bobby's makeup. Wardrobe had dressed him. Bobby was ready to act his part. Ron was sitting in his director's chair giving orders. Everyone moved to their places.

When the final scene of the day was completed, Ron announced, "Your acting was superb today!"

Sheila drove Bobby to his hotel. This time she accepted his invitation to join him for dinner. They looked for Norma as they entered the restaurant.

"I see you looking around. Are you wondering if we'll find Norma here?"

"Yes. She went to Las Vegas to meet a lady friend. She should be back soon. I thought she might be here by now. She sends her regards."

During dinner they discussed the movie, their roles, and how to interpret the director's reactions. Sheila was happy that Ron was so pleased with Bobby. "He's a hard person to satisfy."

"Thanks for all your help and confidence in me."

After dinner, he escorted Sheila to her car, kissed her cheek, and watched her drive away.

*   *   *

The next day, everyone on the set was watching Bobby and Sheila, including Sinclair. He was happy with the film's progress. He invited Bobby, Sheila, Ron, and a few cast members to join him at a dinner gathering that evening. During the cocktail hour, Bobby and Sheila were the subjects of conversation among the partygoers. The gathering ended at one-thirty in the morning. Even though Bobby hadn't wanted to stay late, he enjoyed being recognized by the others in the entertainment world.

*   *   *

Norma was in the hotel room listening to music with a drink in her hand.

"Give me a kiss, Bobby," she begged, and puckered her lips.

He could have been angry but decided he would be gentle and speak softly. He crossed the room, leaned forward, and kissed her cheek.

"How was your day?" she asked in her stupor.

"Great. Mr. Sinclair invited some of the cast to his home for a dinner party and we had a good time. How about you?"

"Oh, it was all right, but I've been a naughty, naughty girl the last few days."

"How so?"

"I got carried away with my gambling again and lost more of your money."

He didn't let on that he had released the marker.

"That's okay if you enjoyed yourself."

"Aren't you even going to ask me how much money I lost?"

"No."

*   *   *

Filming continued for the next few weeks. Bobby was surprised to find Arty sitting in the hotel lounge having a drink with Norma. He kissed her and then took a seat.

"How is the filming coming along?" Arty asked.

"Great, Arty, really great! It's going so well, we may finish shooting ahead of schedule. Ron said we probably have three more weeks."

"Good. Let's see—three weeks. I can begin scheduling a tour on the East coast."

Bobby turned and looked at Norma, who was tapping the stirrer against her glass. He was about to ask her if she had thought about taking that vacation together.

"Okay, Arty. Go ahead."

*   *   *

The film's soundtrack was completed before the deadline. Filming finished within six months—well ahead of schedule. Ron gathered everyone into the large conference room for a final meeting. When it was over, Sheila and Bobby said their good-byes to Ron and Sinclair.

On their way to the parking lot, Bobby and Sheila sat for a few minutes beneath a large shade tree on the studio lot.

"Are you and Norma planning to take a vacation?"

"You know the old saying, No rest for the weary. In fact, my agent is planning a tour on the East coast. What about you?"

"Oh, no real plans except to rest. I'll decide my next move later."

He looked into her eyes. "It's been a wonderful experience for me. And a lot of fun. I owe a lot of the credit to you. I'm sincerely glad I know you."

Sheila let the tears show. "It's been a pleasure for me, too. I hope that we'll meet again, business or pleasure. If ever you're in the area, please give me a call, and maybe we could get together for dinner or a drink. And bring Norma."

They embraced and he kissed her cheek.

*   *   *

They were packed and ready to leave California when Bobby found Norma sitting in the hotel lobby. She held a drink in one hand and the flight schedule in the other, anxious to return to Las Vegas. He ordered a drink for himself and settled into the chair beside her, waiting for the airport shuttle. A bellhop then handed him a portable phone. It was Arty.

"Hi ya, Bobby. I worked out a tour schedule that includes television appearances."

"Okay Arty," he said flatly. "Fill me in."

"You begin a week from Friday. There's this new posh Manhattan club ready to open. The management wants Bobby Shane for a week's engagement. Then there are guest appearances on various television talk shows and a radio show. I have you and Norma booked at the Waldorf Astoria for the month. I'm in the process of making flight arrangements. I'll call you later with all the particulars, okay, Bobby? Have a safe trip."

*   *   *

Norma was excited about staying at the Waldorf. She and Bobby were greeted by a welcoming committee and then led into a private conference room for press interviews.

Between the whirlwind of talk shows and his latest live gig, Bobby had little time to rest. The money he was making seemed to be the motivation to keep going. Arty was elated with his high commission of Bobby's earnings. Norma shopped at the most upscale clothing stores. Bobby didn't approve of her spending sprees, but he was even more concerned about her excessive gambling and drinking.

*   *   *

Bobby was performing at Caesar's Palace when he got word that the premiere of the motion picture was to be at the Graumam's Chinese Theater in one week. He asked Arty to have a placard prepared.

"I need to have someone create a poster that reads: THIS SEAT IS RESERVED IN MEMORY OF LESTER BROWN. I want it placed on the seat next to mine at premiere night, understood?"

"Understood."

* * *

Bobby and Norma arrived in Hollywood the night before the premiere. They checked into the Roosevelt Hotel to be close to the theater. Norma had all ready contacted a special designer to make her evening dress. The studio had arranged a cast luncheon for the day of the premiere.

At twelve-thirty in the afternoon, Norma was still applying her makeup as Bobby nervously waited.

"Norma?"

"I'm coming, I'm coming. Be patient, darling."

He poured himself a drink as he waited and sat by the window while Norma finished preparing for the evening's gala activities.

Suddenly his throat became sore. Norma asked him why he was gargling.

"It's nothing. My throat's a bit sore, but it'll be okay in awhile."

Norma made a spectacular entrance during the cocktail hour. Bobby was delighted with her feminine charm and elegance. She wore a long black dress with a sheer silver-sequined top, a diamond-studded tiara, and long, gold loop earrings.

A hush came over the room when they entered. All eyes were on Bobby and Norma as camera lights flashed continuously. Mr. Sinclair was the first to greet them. Then Sheila walked toward them and extended her hand, "It's a pleasure to meet you, Mrs. Shane. Your husband has told me many nice things about you."

"And I heard many nice things about you, Miss Ross. It's a pleasure to meet you."

Sheila was seated next to Norma at dinner, and they chatted constantly during the entire meal. After the meal, they left to attend the premiere. Along the red carpet, they posed for photographs and answered questions.

Scanning the assembled mass of people, Bobby saw a familiar face in the group. He stood on his tiptoes and stretched his neck to get a better look of the spectator. Everyone noticed they were looking at one other. He broke away from the line of theatergoers and moved directly toward the person.

"Well, well, who do we have here? Mr. Howard of Howard and Wayne Agency. How many other entertainers have you lied to besides me?"

Howard stuttered, "Hello Mr. Shane; nice to see you again."

"I'm not happy to see you. I'll never forget the day you stood me up."

"I'm awfully sorry. I apologize. It was all a misunderstanding."

"A misunderstanding, my ass. That was unprofessional." Bobby vented his long suppressed resentment. Sinclair nudged Bobby to move into the theater.

Bobby was ecstatic when he saw Lester's placard on the seat next to his. He thought it was strange to him that no one questioned it—not even the ever-observant Norma. The room darkened, and the movie began.

When it ended, the audience erupted with applause. Bobby felt that the movie would be a success. He was tired and wanted to return to the hotel. He had to fly to Las Vegas the next day for an evening performance. Norma, on the other hand, loved all the attention, and wanted to stay a little longer.

*　　*　　*

For the next few months the tour continued. Bobby appeared on television and in the nightclub circuit. Arty was watching the money come in while Norma spent her time shopping around Las Vegas and gambling. He often wondered what the circumstances would be if he went bankrupt. How would she handle being poor? He shuddered at the thought.

"Ah, what the hell. It's only money."

One day, Bobby began to feel more tired than usual. He was sure the fast pace had worn him down. His sore throat was now accompanied by frequent headaches. He felt his heart race and he perspired. He had wanted to complain about his health to Arty, and there was no better time than now. Arty came instantly.

"Hi ya, Bobby. What's up?"

"Me, Arty—I'm what's up. It's time for me to take a leave. I'm totally burnt out."

"Are you sure, Bobby? I can work out a few days for you."

Bobby was adamant. "Not days, Arty—weeks. I need to get away to some peace and quiet, where I can unwind."

He gave Bobby a puzzled look. "Sure, whatever you say." He didn't like the idea of losing money, but it was becoming apparent that Bobby was ill, and he did not want to lose his best money-maker.

"Good. When does our current tour end?"

"The end of the week."

"Okay. Ask Stella to book us at a hotel suite in Acapulco. We want to spend two weeks there. And uh,—I never gave Stella and Sol a wedding gift. Give her a week off and book them for a week at the same hotel.

"I'm sure that Stella would appreciate that."

Norma entered the room when she overheard Bobby and Arty arranging the two-week hiatus.

"Yes, I made up my mind. We are going to Mexico. But if you'd rather stay here, it's okay with me."

"I want to go wherever you want to go, darling."

When she kissed her husband on the cheek, it took both men by surprise.

"Okay Arty, that's it. Go to work. And make certain that no one knows about our plans. In fact, make the reservation under the name of Mr. and Mrs. Robert Stone. Is that clear, Arty?"

"Yes sir. Quite clear."

*   *   *

Acapulco is situated around a horseshoe-shaped bay and is surrounded hills and cliffs on both sides. Along the Costera Highway, the main road around the bay, Bobby and Norma passed the busy town square, which is shaded by giant rubber and mango trees. On the left side, the square is lined with sidewalk cafes. To their right, the bay is lined with beaches.

In the hotel lobby, Bobby noticed Stella and Sol standing at the reservation desk. When Stella saw Bobby, she smiled and waved.

"Hi, Bobby. Where's Norma?"

Bobby pointed toward one of the lobby's high-backed chairs. He called to Norma. "Come on over and say hello."

They talked for a short while and made plans to meet for dinner.

*   *   *

Bobby was happy during the first week of his vacation. It was also the first time he had traveled to a place where he wasn't recognized. For him and Norma, it was their belated honeymoon. They had a week's worth of relaxing on the beaches, eating on the veranda, and lovemaking.

But the leisurely vacation was cut short during the second week when he sensed that Norma had begun to get restless. She was homesick for the Las Vegas excitement, and for being noticed as Mrs. Bobby Shane. And she missed her biggest passion—gambling.

An invitation was extended to Irma to join them at the hotel for a few days. She happily accepted and was there in a matter of hours. The two friends shopped in many stores along the busy Costera highway.

For Bobby, the two weeks went by quickly. Norma was happy it was over.

*　　*　　*

Bobby was in demand again. He had been booked for a four-week stint in Las Vegas before his vacation started. A month later, he opened a two-week singing engagement at a posh New York club. But his health became progressively worse. He spent almost every evening gargling salt water to relieve a sore throat, and he took over-the-counter medications.

In the meantime, his first motion picture became a financial success.

Bobby was offered several movie scripts. To Arty's surprise, he didn't seem interested and turn them all down.

*　　*　　*

Through the bathroom walls, Norma heard Bobby gargling in the bathroom

"Is there something wrong with your throat? You've been gargling a lot recently"

"It's a little sore. I'm probably catching a cold.

"You'd better see a doctor if it persists."

"Sure, in the morning," he said to appease her.

*　　*　　*

He stopped at a pharmacy on his way to the hotel and purchased a variety of throat medications. The lobby's men's room was a convenient place to gargle before meeting Norma. He had not wanted to argue with her about seeing a doctor. He slid the bottle into his coat pocket, pulled out a lozenge, and then went directly to the pool, where he knew he would find Norma sunbathing.

"No work today?" Norma asked.

"No. I thought that I'd give you a treat and spend the afternoon with you."

"That'll be the day," she teased. "Now tell me what's wrong?"

"You mean it shows?"

"That's putting it mildly."

"Any pain?"

"A little."

"All right then, take a hot bath. I'll prepare one of my mother's old fashioned remedies."

Bobby soaked in a hot, steamy bath until Norma came in with a glass of her homemade concoction and told him to gargle and swallow. He took the glass in hand and sniffed it.

What the hell is this, Norma? It smells awful."

"Gargle," she insisted. "It's more effective when it's hot."

He reluctantly took a small sip. "Phew. Are you kidding me? After this, I won't have to worry about singing ever again."

"Finish every drop," she insisted. "Then get in bed for a good night's sleep." She rubbed his throat and neck with a vapor rub, which seemed to give him some relief. He soon fell asleep.

*   *   *

The phone rang and Norma rushed to answer it before Bobby woke up.

"Norma? Arty here. Charlie tells me that Bobby isn't feeling well— has a sore throat or something and has been ordered to bed."

"Hello, Arty. Yes, he has a sore throat, but the doctor diagnosed it as possible strain. He should be all right in a day or two."

"That's great. I got a little worried. When he wakes up, tell him I will be flying in tonight and I'll stop in to see him, okay?"

"Yes, Arty. Thanks for calling.

*   *   *

The next day, Bobby felt worse. A crew member suggested that he see an ear, nose, and throat specialist. An appointment was made for the next day with Dr. James C. Whitman, an otolaryngologist at University General Hospital. Arty went along. Bobby spent most of the day going through a lengthy examination that included having blood drawn, a throat swab, an ultrasound of the throat, and chest X-rays.

"What does it look like, Doc?"

"I'd only be speculating. I realize how you feel, but I'd much rather be sure before I tell you anything."

Several days later, Dr. Whitman gave Bobby the news.

"I have some bad news for you. The test results indicate there is a large thyroid nodule pressing against your larynx and causing irritation. It appears to be benign, but we need to take a biopsy sample to test the tissue for malignancy before I make a diagnosis and prescribe treatment."

Bobby was stunned, and sat silent for a few minutes while he absorbed what the doctor had said.

"A what?"

"You have a large growth, very close to your vocal chords. In order to find out if there are any cancer cells present, the growth must be removed. Removing the growth is the number one priority, and the sooner the better."

"But you said removal. Shouldn't that fix it?"

"True. That means the growth needs to be removed or it may continue to grow and present further complications."

"Like what complications?"

"Like causing you to lose your voice altogether. So no more singing for now. Your throat needs to avoid irritation."

"How long, Doc? How long will I be laid up?"

"Recuperation from the surgery will not take more than a week. Not being in the motion picture business, I really can't say how it will affect your acting career; that would be up to the studio experts. As for singing, I'm sorry, but I don't see you singing in the future."

"Wow, Doc, you're full of good tidings, aren't you?"

"Having to give bad news is part of being a physician."

Bobby managed to compose himself and walked from the doctor's office into the waiting room where Arty had been sitting.

"Oy vey!" Arty exclaimed when he heard the news. He put his hands to his cheeks and felt his financial world crumbling. Later, Arty relayed the news to Charlie.

* * *

Bobby couldn't find Norma when he returned to the room. She hadn't left a note explaining where she had gone. *Just as well*, he thought. He wanted to be alone to think about his dilemma. In his room he sat on the bed and pondered his future. *Where do I go from here?*

He walked onto the patio, took a deep breath, and gazed out at the landscape. He watched as children ran around, enjoying themselves without a worry in the world. If only they could realize how good they have it. He looked up at the bright blue sky and tears welled in his eyes. He thought about his life—where he had been and where he was now. He thought about growing up in Cincinnati with his childhood friend, Mary; and about Lester Brown, the paunchy, gray-haired piano player who agreed to be his accompanist. He chuckled bitter sweetly when he thought about the little guy with a wrinkled face, and how he died so suddenly.

"Lester, where did I go wrong? Why is this happening to me?" he spoke aloud.

"Who are you talking to?" Norma asked. She had quietly returned and heard Bobby on the patio.

"No one. Just thinking out loud. I have something to tell you, Norma."

"Not now, dear, I have to shower and dress. I'm going out. Be a dear and have dinner brought up for yourself."

The bathroom door closed before he had a chance to speak. He thought of Mary and wondered what his life would have been like had he married her? Sweet, devoted, undemanding Mary.

I'm sure life would be a lot easier, he thought. A kid or two, maybe. Hell it's too late to even think about it. She's probably married by now. I can't dwell on it."

CHAPTER 9

Norma returned from her night out late in the evening.

"Bobby, look at the buy I got on this outfit." She held it against her body.

"Norma, please sit. I need to tell you something. Look, you are going to listen and listen good. My throat is a lot worse than I thought. I have some crazy growth. I forget the medical term. Anyway, the doctor told me that I am done as a singer."

Norma's mouth dropped open and her eyes widened as she looked at him. "What are you saying?" she screamed. "He must be wrong! How can that studio doctor tell you that you are done as singer?"

"No. Not him."

Bobby explained that he had gone to a throat specialist who took extensive tests, and how he had received the results that morning

Norma's reacted like someone in denial. She wasn't convinced that he had gone to the best doctor. She reached for the telephone.

"Forget it. I've already seen the best," he told her.

She saw an end to her lavish lifestyle "How are we going to pay the bills?"

"Damn it, Norma, is that all you can think about at a time like this?"

"Well, I'm sorry. But I'm used to nice things, and nice things cost money."

"We should have invested our money instead of spending it. We would live well from the profit and dividends. I can always get a job, Norma. We can make it—I know we can. We have to cut back, that's all."

"Cut back?! Over my dead body!" She pushed him aside, threw her suit to the floor, and rushed away.

* * *

Bobby anguished over Norma's spending sprees, nightly gambling, and heavy drinking. She provoked him in every way she could. He tried his best to ignore her, but they fought constantly. She wanted one thing— a divorce, and the large monetary settlement she expected would come with it.

* * *

Bobby had decided to go ahead with the operation. The surgery was successful—no malignancy found.

He awoke to find Dr. Whitman standing by his bedside.

"You made the right decision. It was about to become malignant, but we got it in time. How do you feel?"

"Pretty good, Doc." he whispered. "But I'm not ready to sing just yet."

Dr. Whitman enjoyed the wit. "Your throat will be sore for a little while."

"When do you think I'll be able to leave the hospital, doc?"

"In a few days. It depends on how well you recuperate. When you stop bleeding, the drain will be removed. Don't push it. If you do not recover properly, you could have adhesions and scar tissue."

"OK, Doc. Anything you say."

Two days later, the drain was removed. Bobby couldn't wait to get out of the hospital. He checked out that weekend.

* * *

One night, Norma came home intoxicated. That put Bobby over the edge. He lost control and slapped her around. A neighbor who had overheard the fight called the authorities. Bobby was taken into custody, fined for disturbing the peace, placed on probation, and had a peace bond filed against him with the domestic court. Norma had been taken to the hospital to treat her injuries.

Norma's attorney had photographs of the mistreated and bruised celebrity's wife.

The tabloids carried the episode on their front pages. Norma was well on her way toward a divorce for spousal abuse and irreconcilable differences.

The divorce proceedings went in Norma's favor. Bobby was ordered to pay Norma four-and-a-half million dollars, plus fifty thousand per month, to be canceled if Norma were ever to remarry.

Bobby tried to protest the decision. "That's not fair, your honor. That will wipe me out, and I have to support myself and pay for my operation."

The judge hammered the bench with his gavel, "Order in the court. You are out of order, Mr. Shane. If you continue to disrupt this hearing, I will hold you in contempt. As your attorney knows, Mr. Shane, you have the right to an appeal.

Bobby walked out of the courthouse and took a breath of fresh air. *At least I'm free of her. I'm a free man.*

CHAPTER 10

The four-day train ride from Las Vegas to New York City wasn't exactly pleasant. Passengers had gawked at him; others asked for his autograph. Once the excitement passed, he settled down in a cramped, uncomfortable seat. While looking at the passing countryside, he thought about Norma. He had married for love, but his original infatuation and lust had dissipated once she filed for divorce. He had been phenomenally successful in fulfilling his dream of becoming a professional singer. She had been calculating and ruthlessly took him for all she could get. Arty was right—she was as cold as ice cubes.

Bobby stared at the giant clock hanging in the center of Pennsylvania station. It was 6 a.m. when he walked onto 8th Avenue into a dark, dreary, chilly October morning. He was back to where it all began. The streets were relatively quiet at this hour. The early morning rush hour hadn't begun, though vendors were busy setting up their wares.

He walked to 42nd Street. Broadway looked different. It appeared to be a much smaller place with its windows and doors shuttered.

He checked into the Manhattan Manor hotel and unpacked his bags while he awaited a decent time to call Arty.

"Arty Mann Agency, how can I help you?"

"Hi, Stella, it's me Bobby."

"Hi, sweetie. Nice hearing from you. Are you calling from the West coast?"

"No, I arrived in New York this morning. I took a room at the Manhattan Manor Hotel."

"Sorry about your illness. You'll make a comeback though, if I know you."

"How's Sol?"

"He's doing great, thank you."

"I'm happy for you. Is your boss in?"

"No, Bobby, he went up town with Charlie. He should be back shortly, though. I'll tell him you called. Let me have your phone number and I'll—"

"That's okay, Stella. I'll sneak up on him in a day or two. Don't mention that I called."

"All right, Bobby. Talk to you later."

Bobby took his medication, soaked in a hot tub of water, and then stretched out on the bed for a much needed rest. He slept until early the next morning.

After breakfast, Bobby walked to the Pink Swan Club, where he found Mr. Gordon working in his office. Gordon asked about his plans.

"I don't know what the future holds for me. I can't sing anymore, and what money I had was awarded to my ex-wife. Well, almost all of it. I was able to keep a few dollars."

"That's a shame." Gordon said as he bit into a bagel. For a brief moment, Gordon thought about hiring him, but was too embarrassed to offer him the job he had available. He offered him his best wishes instead.

Before he left the club, Bobby slowly wandered around and stopped at center stage. He focused on the room's empty tables and imagined himself singing to a group of patrons.

"This is where I got my start," he thought as he sucked in a deep breath. This is where it all began."

*   *   *

After dinner, he went to the hotel's cocktail lounge and ordered bourbon. He wondered if he should be having the drink.

The bartender sat the glass and then asked, "Say, aren't you Bobby Shane?"

"Sorry to say that I am."

"I thought so. You put on a great show—my wife and I saw three of them. You're a great singer."

He refilled Bobby's glass several times, "On the house, Mr. Shane."

The next morning, Bobby had a slight hangover and a very sore throat. He stood in front of a mirror and opened his mouth wide to have a look.

Must be catching a cold, he told himself. *Surely, the alcohol couldn't have caused the pain.*

* * *

Bobby walked into the nearest bank to seek employment. He had been an accounting clerk in Cincinnati before he embarked on a singing career. The receptionist immediately recognized him and was captivated.

"Mr. Shane! Can I help you?" She pushed her long hair off her shoulder with the back of her hand as she tried to keep her composure.

He forced a smile. "Yes, I would like to speak with someone about a job."

"Yes sir! Follow me to Mr. Hurst's office—he's the manager."

She led him through a narrow corridor to Mr. Hurst's corner office.

"Mr. Hurst—Mr. Shane is looking for a job."

Mr. Hurst looked young enough to be in his mid-twenties. He received Bobby with an extended hand and offered him a seat. Mr. Hurst was used to talking to celebrities, but he was fascinated as to why a well-known entertainer would want to work in a bank.

"So, you're looking for a job. Any experience working in a bank Mr. Shane?"

"I worked as an accounting clerk for about two years, and I am very good at figures and—"

Mr. Hurst was about to explain the available employment opportunities when he noticed the female employees sneaking peeks and causing a commotion.

"I'm sorry, Mr. Shane; I have nothing available now. But if you leave your resume, I'll notify you of any openings."

It didn't take Bobby long to realize that he might have had a job if it hadn't been for his popularity. No doubt, he would have caused a disruption.

"Thank you for your time, Mr. Hurst."

After walking for most of the day, his throat began to feel tight. As a precaution, he stopped at a convenience store for throat lozenges, a cup of coffee, and a sandwich. After taking one bite he tossed it into the trash container for the pain of swallowing.

The following day, he was up at nine. The lozenges seemed to help his throat feel a little better. Looking at himself in the mirror, an idea crossed his mind. *I'll change my appearance. Dye and restyle my hair. Perhaps grow a moustache, even a beard*, he told himself.

Within a week, Bobby had begun his metamorphosis. The hair that once touched his collar had been cut short, and he grew a beard and mustache. After weeks of unsuccessful job searching, his morale dwindled. His only consolation was that no one recognized him. He called Arty.

"Hi Stella, Bobby here. Is your boss in this time?"

In the background he heard Arty say, "I'm in Chicago. Tell him I'm in Chicago."

Disheartened, he put the phone back in its cradle.

One knows one's friends when one is in a crisis. I always knew Arty was a shrewd businessman, but I thought of him as a friend, too.

He purchased a bottle of bourbon to drown his sorrows. Money problems were weighing on his mind. His funds were running out. He needed a reprieve and he needed to look for cheaper accommodations. He had become used to living in hotels. During his singing career, he moved from hotel to hotel, but those days were over.

He sat on the bed and looked around the room. He wondered if his luck was going to change for the better.

He suddenly decided to throw caution to the wind and try to get a singing job. He'd look for a small café, so that he would not have to strain his voice.

He showered, shaved, and dressed. He walked around the Village in search of the perfect venue.

*   *   *

He entered a club that seemed appropriate. He noticed a piano on a small bandstand. It was crowded. He approached the bartender.

"Excuse me, is the manager around? I'm a singer looking for a job. I thought that maybe you could use some entertainment."

"Just a minute." The bartender retreated to a back room. He emerged a few moments later.

"Mr. Rose is the first door on the right."

"What's your handle, kid?" Mr. Rose asked.

"Bobby Shane."

"Oh yeah, the singer with the throat problem."

"I'm feeling much better. No problem at all."

"Sure. Tell you what—I'll give you a shot. Be here tomorrow night at eight. If you do well, I'll put you on indefinitely. Can't pay you much—say a grand a night."

"It's a start, Mr. Rose."

*　　*　　*

Bobby arrived at the club at eight. He immediately noticed the makeshift sign on the bay window that read: BOBBY SHANE RETURNS. He was giddy when he saw the crowd gathered in the club—not a table to be had. His fans were there in force. Bobby was introduced to the piano player, who was given the portfolio containing Bobby's sheet music. After coordinating his music with the piano player, he was ready.

Mr. Rose addressed the audience.

"Ladies and Gentlemen, the management proudly present the one and only Bobby Shane, who is making his long-awaited comeback. Let's welcome him with a great big round of applause—Bobby Shane!"

His first few numbers went rather well. The crowd stood on their feet, applauding. In his final half hour, Bobby became overconfident and decided to give the crowd songs that required him to sing at his highest octave. He approached the piano player and said, "Miss You Tonight", A-sharp."

"You sure? That's a very high note."

"Play it."

"Okay, it's your throat."

Halfway thru the song, Bobby felt a sharp pain in his throat, which soon became unbearable. He managed to finish his final song of the first show. He hurried to his dressing room, spitting up blood.

As they waited, the crowd asked for more. Mr. Rose approached the microphone and explained that since it was Bobby's first show in quite a while, he had to take it slow. "He will return on stage shortly for his second show."

But that was not to be. Not even gargling with warm salt water could help. He continued spitting up blood.

Mr. Rose rushed to Bobby's dressing room and saw Bobby spitting up blood in the sink.

"I thought you said that you were completely healed."

"I'm sorry. It's not going to work as I believed."

"What the hell are you telling me? You told me that everything was fine, and the operation fixed your throat."

"I thought so too. I shouldn't have tried hitting the high notes."

"High notes, low notes—who gives a damn? You have to do a second show. I kept my part of the bargain; now you have to keep yours."

"I'm sorry, but I just can't. Look, you don't owe me a dime for the first show, okay?"

"Look, wise guy; there are people out there paying good money to see a show. You're going out there!"

"I'm sorry," he said as he prepared to leave.

Rose called for three men. "This bastard refuses to do the second show. Maybe we can persuade him to perform."

The first blow felt like a sledgehammer. Bobby crumbled to the floor on his knees. Rose yelled, "Okay, enough! Throw the bastard out, and use the back entrance."

Bobby hit the back alley with a thud. He slowly picked himself up and stumbled home. A small article made the entertainment section of the News: Bobby Shane attempt at comeback fails.

Friday morning, Bobby packed his belongings and checked out of the hotel.

*　　*　　*

"Where to, buddy?" the cab driver asked. Bobby gave him Slade's address.

Soon after he arrived at the familiar building, he thought, *Ah, it's the same as I remember it.*

Slade had been sweeping when the cab pulled up. Bobby burst out onto the sidewalk.

"Hi, Mr. Slade, do you remember me? Bobby Shane."

"Ah yes—my star boarder. What can I do for you?"

"I'm looking for a furnished room with reasonable rates. Do you have any vacancies, Mr. Slade?"

"No, I'm sorry. All the rooms are rented."

Bobby turned toward the cab but Slade stopped him.

"Wait a minute, hold on there. I do have a very small first floor room. It's across the hall from me. I use it for storage. It even has a bathroom. I'll move some furniture in for you."

"I'll take it."

He removed his belongings from the cab and followed Mr. Slade to his new apartment. The door opened to a room cluttered with boxes. It was dingy and unattractive. Bobby handed Slade the rent money.

*   *   *

Two weeks had passed and Bobby still hadn't found a job. His medication was gone. During one of his daily walks, he found a restaurant advertising for a dishwasher.

"$250 a week, including meals," said Mr. Leech, the owner. "The hours are five to eleven, six days a week. You can start now."

"Thanks, Mr. Leech. I'll do a good job for you."

"I'm sure you will, Mr. Payne." Bobby used a false name to keep his true identity hidden.

"Oscar!" Mr. Leech yelled.

A young man emerged from the kitchen. He was a short and skinny, with spiky blonde hair and a long nose.

"Yes sir, Mr. Leech."

"Bobby is our new dishwasher. Give him a uniform and a hat. Help him get familiar with the dishwasher and explain the routine."

"Yes sir, Mr. Leech." Then he turned to Bobby. "Hi, my name is Oscar."

"Hi Oscar, I'm Bobby."

Oscar gave Bobby a stained uniform and a large white apron. His hat looked like a shower cap. He was expected to scrape dirty dishes, give them a quick rinse at the double sink, and then stack them in the dishwasher. Once washed, they were to be removed and set out for re-use.

Not an hour of his shift had gone by when he felt someone brush by him. He looked back to see one of the waitresses standing behind him.

"Sorry, Mr. Payne. I'm Kay."

He watched as she picked up a large tray of food, and walked toward the swinging door. She pushed it open with her free arm and disappeared into the dining room. A few minutes later, she had returned to get another tray of orders. She saw him watching her and smiled.

"You married or single?" she asked, peering at him through sparkling blue eyes.

"Pleasure to meet you, Kay. I'm married."

She quickly returned to her waitressing.

It had been a long six hours. Bobby's legs were weak from standing, his back ached from bending over, and his hands were raw. Hot soapy water dripped from his rubber gloves. He replaced his uniform and cap with his coat, and bid farewell to Oscar.

*   *   *

When four o'clock came around again, Bobby wasn't feeling well, even through he had slept late. He began his second day as a dishwasher. Mr. Leech approached him.

"Well, Bobby, how are things going?"

"Fine, Mr. Leech, just fine."

"Good. Since you're set up and things are slow right now, you might as well have dinner. The chef's daily special is prime rib with baked potato."

"Okay, thanks."

Even though the waitresses believed he was married with children, they didn't care. They began spending more and more time in the kitchen chatting with Bobby. There was something magnetic about him. Oscar tried to defend him.

"Come on, girls, leave him be. He has work to do. There will be hell to pay if Leech catches you."

But the attention finally got to Mr. Leech. "I'm sorry, Mr. Payne, but I have to let you go."

"But why? Aren't I doing a good job?" Bobby asked.

"You're a good worker, but your being here is creating a disruption among the other employees. It's easier to get a dishwasher than to find a good waitress. Oscar is a super chef and the waitresses are good at keeping the patrons happy."

"Well, thanks for the opportunity anyway, Mr. Leech."

"Sorry it didn't work out."

Bobby received his pay and left.

CHAPTER 11

Bobby was back on 42nd Street, where he saw it: ARTY MANN THEATRICAL AGENCY in big bright lights. He walked into the building. There at the front desk was Stella along with two other girls working at their computers.

"Bobby!" She ran up to him and kissed his cheek. "How are you?"

"Great, Stell. You look sexy as always. Is Arty in?"

"He's in his office with two gentlemen."

Bobby looked around the office again. "Doing all right for himself, eh Stell?"

"Yes, quite all right for himself. I'm sorry that he was not in when you called, but you know-"

"No problem, Stell. I understand."

At that very moment, the two well-dressed men came out of the office, followed by Arty.

"Well, well, if it isn't Bobby Shane. How are you?"

Bobby could see his hand trembling as he offered it.

"Gentlemen, you remember Bobby Shane?"

They exchanged pleasantries with Bobby and left.

"Come in, Bobby. What'll you have to drink—your usual?"

"No thanks." Bobby eyed the luxurious office. "Things have gotten pretty good for you."

"Yeah, finally got lucky. I have an appointment in thirty minutes, but for you I'll cancel it. Stella!"

"Yes, Mr. Mann?"

"Cancel that appointment with Mr. Bassett until five o'clock."

"What?"

"You know, Mr. Bassett. Mr. *Bassett*." He winked.

"Oh, that Mr. Bassett. Yes sir, right away." She rolled her eyes as she passed Bobby.

Bobby grinned and shook his head.

"How about that, Bobby. We can talk awhile."

"Sure, thanks," he said as he played Arty's game. His eyes followed Stella out the door; Arty noticed.

"Yes sir, our little Stella's married. She's really happy, too. I hope for her sake it's the real thing this. So what's up?" Arty pointed to his throat. "Any chance of singing again?"

"Get off it. You know darn well I had to give up singing."

"Right, that's right. Sure is tough—just when you were on top."

"Have you seen Norma around lately?"

"Seen her plenty. The day after you left for New York, she seemed down in the dumps and vanished for about a month. Then out of the clear blue, she was in the club gambling—really high stakes. I hear that she blew most of the money she got from your divorce settlement in no time.

"So what? It was her money."

"Hold on, Bobby—you asked me."

"I know, but you don't have to give her all the blame. Go on."

"That's about it. What else can I tell you?"

"How about men?"

"Oh, now I get it. Still carrying the torch, eh?"

"No, just wondering."

"She didn't change at all. She still has that beautiful keister. Funny though, I don't remember seeing her out with many guys."

"Thanks for your time. See you around."

"Could I offer you a few bucks? You know, just for old times. Things really aren't going as good as they look for me."

"Sure, I noticed," Bobby said as he looked at the new girls typing away.

"Aw, they're just trainees from the typing school. I give them a few bucks—you know, donations."

"Sure Arty, I understand. You don't owe me a thing."

On the way out, Bobby stopped by Stella's desk. "Well Stell, it was nice seeing you again." Bobby kissed her cheek and left.

*   *   *

On 48th street, Bobby saw a Help Wanted sign at Irvin's Manufacturing. He took the stairs to the second floor and opened the door to a brightly lit room filled with noisy sewing and pressing machines. A sign directed him to Mr. Grim, office manager of the human resources department.

"Do you have experience pressing garments, Mr. Payne?" Grim asked.

"Yes sir—five years to be exact."

"Where did you work last?"

He hesitated for a moment before answering. "Shane Clothing Company in Ohio."

"Good. Can you start tomorrow morning at seven-thirty sharp?"

"Yes sir—seven-thirty,"

"Piece work affects your salary, that should be familiar to you. It's up to you how much you earn. You will receive forty cents for each piece you finish, ok?"

"Great, Mr. Grim. I was only making thirty cents in Ohio."

*   *   *

The next morning, Bobby arrived for work and reported to Mr. Grim.

"Ready to start work, Mr. Payne?"

"Ready as I'll ever be."

They walked the back of the plant to the pressing machines.

"Here we are, Mr. Payne. This will be your machine and this hamper will be stocked with garments at all times. Currently, we are making coats. When you complete each coat, hang them on this rack. The floor boy will do the rest. Tear off the stub from each ticket, and turn it in at the end of the day so that we know how much to pay you. Good luck."

"Excuse me, Mr. Grim. Will someone show me how you want the coats pressed?"

"No, routine finishing." Mr. Grim continued his rounds.

"Yes sir." *Well, Bobby, you really screwed up this time.*

He turned to a short fellow working next to him.

"Excuse me, I'm new here. Would you be so kind and start my machine?"

"Sure. My name's Jimmy."

"I'm Bobby. Nice to meet you."

He watched Jimmy for a while, and then tried his hand. He placed the coat on the pressing board, released the steam control, drove the board down onto the coat, and held it there. He did not know what lever to use to release the board and the coat began to burn.

Jimmy jumped to his aid.

"Thanks. I'm not familiar with this type of machine. Oh, to hell with it," Bobby stomped off to Grim's office.

"I'm sorry, Mr. Grim, I lied to you. I don't know one thing about pressing. I needed a job."

Grim was sympathetic. "Tell you what—if you're really hurting for a job, I could use a floor boy. All you have to do is make certain that the tailors and pressers always have garments to work with. Keep the hampers full. Later on, I'll teach you to be a presser. It only pays two hundred and fifty dollars a week."

"You got a deal, Mr. Grim. I'll take it."

*　　*　　*

Bobby was really enjoying his modest paying job. His diet was healthier and he finally had a bit of money.

When the noon whistle sounded, he went to the mobile lunch truck.

"Egg salad, please, and chocolate milk."

He walked to the far corner, sat on a parked flatbed truck, and proceeded to enjoy his lunch. Three young girls walked to where Bobby was sitting. All three were attractive and appeared to be in their early twenties.

"Hi, there," one of them said.

"Hi yourself."

"How do you like working here?"

"I like it just fine." He took a bite of his sandwich.

"My name is Charlotte. This is Ann, and that's Rita."

"Pleasure, I'm Bobby Sh—Payne,"

"Care for some of my homemade cake?" Ann asked.

"Sure, thanks."

"You're not from New York, are you?"

"No, I'm originally from Ohio."

"What made you choose this type of a job?"

"Well, the only other trade that I know is the restaurant business. I had my diner here in New York but it didn't pan out." Bobby really laid it on. "As you may know, you have to take whatever you can get to support a wife and six kids."

"Six kids? Wow-ee!" Ann howled. "You're married?"

"Yes. Going on fifteen years now."

"I need to make a phone call."

The other girls also made excuses to get away.

Bobby laughed to himself. *Strange*, he thought. Despite his love for sex, he wasn't interested in them. Getting his life back together was his priority. The whistle blew, signaling the end of lunch.

*   *   *

For the next three months, Bobby did his job and learned how to press clothes. He couldn't have been happier. One day he was summoned to see Mr. Grim. Bobby walked into his office, wondering why he had been requested.

"Hi, Bobby. I'm sorry to inform you that I'll have to lay you off."

"I thought I was doing a good job, Mr. Grim."

"You're doing a great job. However, you're caught up in a numbers game. What I mean is—business is slowing down. In order to keep ahead, we must cut our payroll."

"I understand, Mr. Grim. When?"

"The end of the week."

*   *   *

On his way home after his last day of work, the rain came down hard. He took shelter at the luncheonette where he and Stella had breakfast the day he met Tommy Simms.

"Coffee—cream and sugar, please."

"Anything else?" the waitress asked.

"No, thanks; that's it."

The waitress returned a few moments later. "Here, you are, sir."

"Just a minute, please."

"Yes sir?"

"Tell me, there was a fellow who worked here a while back."

"You mean Tommy?"

"That's right—Tommy."

"He left about a month ago. Claimed he was going to make millions with a show he is producing. Is that all, sir? I'm kind of busy."

"Sure, thanks a lot." Bobby finished his coffee and left.

*   *   *

Life had become mere survival for Bobby.

Maybe, I should pack it in and head back home to Cincinnati. Nah, no good. I still have to find a job, and things aren't any better there either.

Feeling low, he hit the first bar he came to and drank his supper. Three hours later, he was feeling no pain. He bought a bottle to take with him and staggered to his apartment

*   *   *

In her office at the Hendricks Fashion Company, Mary had been hard at work. During her breaks, she read everything that was written about Bobby. After all these years, she still carried a torch for him. She had loved him ever since childhood.

She leaned back in her chair and turned toward the picture window to view the New York skyline. She wondered why he hadn't tried to contact her. She concluded that he would probably not want her pity, especially since she had succeeded in her job and had become a board member.

Mary had many opportunities to date available bachelors, but whenever she considered her social life, Bobby would flash across her mind. She had taken a couple of days off to look for him. Down deep in her heart, she felt that he must have needed her. She wondered if he was living in the same apartment he showed her when she first came to New York.

*   *   *

Bobby was awakened by the sun shining in his eyes. It was 10:15 a.m. He found a glass and filled it with bourbon and water.

CHAPTER 12

Despite gargling with warm salt water and sucking cough drops, Bobby's throat had gotten worse. He drank morning, noon, and night. Because of the pain, he often skipped meals. He snacked on chicken soup and crackers.

One morning, he desperately needed a drink. At noon the package store would be open. He splashed water on his unshaven face and left his apartment.

He made certain Mr. Slade wasn't around. In his delirium, he didn't know if his rent was in arrears. As he was walking, he realized he was out of money. He decided to pawn his watch.

As he opened the door of the Three Ball Pawn Shop, the loud jingling of the door resounded in his head. Immediately, Bobby sensed he was in trouble. The guy sitting behind the glass counter was smoking a cigar, and he looked tough as nail. He wasn't mistaken. The pawnbroker gave him twenty dollars for his expensive watch. He went to the package store and bought what he needed.

It wasn't long before half of the bottle was gone. In his stupor, he tried singing. After hitting the high note, he grasped his throat.

Damn you, Bobby. You're a ding-a-ling. Raising the bottle high he announced, "Here's a toast to the best singer this side of nowhere."

The booze had been taking its toll on his health. He became ill with dry heaves and often had terrible headaches. Occasionally he blacked out. When he needed money for booze, he pawned his jewelry and clothing.

With the money he received, he refilled his cache of hard liquor, soup, and crackers.

* * *

The knock on the door felt like a jab in his brain. He staggered to the door.

It's probably Slade, looking for the rent.

"Hello, Mr. Slade. About the rent, I-"

"No need," he interrupted. "She already paid your rent. You're good for the next six months."

"Who? Who was she?"

"She said she is your sister."

"Mary? Was it Mary? Did she enter the apartment?"

"Yes, I let her in with my master key. One foot through the door, she grabbed my arm. I thought the poor girl was going to faint. I wanted to wake you, but she insisted that you sleep."

* * *

For the next few days, he continued to drink and skip meals. Bobby was inebriated for hours at a time. He started to spit up blood, and used the booze as a painkiller.

He stared at the ceiling and thought of Mary seeing him at his worst.

I have to move immediately.

He finished half of his last bottle, packed the remainder of his clothes, and put his key under Slade's door. Then he staggered to the sidewalk.

CHAPTER 13

People shook their heads in disgust and pity when they saw Bobby. Some offered him money, but he ignored them. He ended up in the Bowery, known for being home to vagrants. One of them grabbed him by the arm.

"Hey, buddy row, got a short snifter?"

Bobby made the mistake of revealing his nearly empty bottle of bourbon. Like vultures, they grabbed his bottle and passed it around until it was empty.

Suddenly they were in a hurry to leave. The last one with the bottle said, "Let's go or we'll miss out."

"Miss out on what?" Bobby asked as he followed along.

"Chow, man—chow at the Mission. Soup and sandwiches."

Bobby started chugging faster. The soup was watery, but it was hot and tasted good.

"You're new at this, ain't you, kid?" asked the older fellow.

Bobby stayed silent.

"Don't want to answer, eh? Okay, stick with me. I'll take care of you. I'm Sammy. What's yours?"

"Bob," he whispered with his raspy voice.

"Pleasure." Sammy extended his hand.

"Do you have any dough, Bob?" he whispered.

Bobby put his hand in his pocket. "Seven dollars and change."

"Good. There's a flophouse, half a buck a night. The bed is small and the mattress is filled with straw, but it's warm."

*   *   *

The flophouse was an old two-story frame house with few windows. It contained forty metal-framed beds. It was hot and crowded. The horrible stench of body odor was too much for Bobby; he wanted to vomit.

"Don't let it bother you, kid; you'll get used to it," Sammy assured him.

*   *   *

Sammy woke Bobby up early the next morning.

"Okay kid, you got your fifty cents worth. Check out time. Let's beat those bums to the Mission for coffee and doughnuts."

When they got there, the line was short.

"How about that, kid?" Sammy gave him the elbow. "Fourth and fifth in line. Not bad, huh?"

Bobby nodded his approval.

When they finished their breakfast Sammy announced, "Time to go to work, kid," Bobby looked at him, perplexed.

"No, nothing like hard labor. Come on, I'll show you."

*   *   *

On 42nd Streets, they started walking along the curb.

"Head down," Sammy ordered. "You never know what you may find on the sidewalk. That's the secret. Ah, there's a big one." He picked up a cigar butt and lit it. He took a deep drag and blew the smoke up toward the sky. "Tastes just great. Puff, kid?"

Bobby shook his head. It made him sick just watching Sammy put the cigar butt in his mouth.

"Stay close to me and we'll have lunch soon."

Bobby didn't say a word, preferring to just follow close behind.

"Say, buddy, do you have any change for a cup of coffee?" Sammy asked a passerby.

"Beat it, bum." Three more people gave them the same answer.

"Don't worry, kid; we'll make it."

By twelve-thirty, they had acquired only one dollar and fifty cents.

"Can't understand it," Sammy pouted. "My luck is normally better than this."

"It's me," Bobby mumbled. "Bad luck Charlie."

"Nah, I don't believe in nonsense like that. Tell you what—we have just enough for a small snifter. How about if we call it a day? It's your first day and all. We'll skip lunch and wet our whistles instead."

Bobby nodded.

"That's the spirit. We'll make it big tomorrow, wait and see."

They walked into the nearest bar. "Two whiskies, please."

A tall, muscular bartender brought them a bottle. "Two bucks in advance," he said.

"What? Don't you trust us?"

"I trust none of you bums."

Bobby was ready to punch him out, but Sammy grabbed him by the seat of his pants. "He's not worth dirtying your hands over, Bob. Drink up." Sammy put a dollar-fifty on the bar and looked at Bobby for the rest. Bobby placed his fifty cents on the bar.

Bobby gulped his drink in one swig. Not being used to the cheap stuff, he almost gagged. He could hardly speak. Sammy patted him on the back a few times and laughed. "You have to get used to this junk, kid. That's what you get for a dollar a shot. You have to ease it down, you know? Baby it."

Before Bobby had a chance to recover, the bartender walked over. "Same?"

"Like to," Sammy answered, "but all the loot's gone. Can you give us fifty cents' worth?"

"All right, beat it. Go beg somewhere else."

Bobby couldn't hold back any longer and cut loose with a right hook to the chops. The guy didn't budge an inch.

"Let's get the hell out of here!" Sammy yelled.

But Bobby was not quick enough. The bartender grabbed him by the back of his shirt collar and dragged him along to the end of the bar. He punched Bobby in the face and sent him sailing to the sidewalk.

"What the hell hit me?" Bobby asked.

"That's something else I'm gonna have to teach you. Let's go to the Mission. By the time we walk it, supper will be ready."

As he staggered along, Bobby used his shirt to wipe the blood from his mouth. "That bastard."

"Calm down; you'll be all right. Do you have any dough left?"

Bobby dug deep in both pockets and came up with two bucks.

"Good, we'll pick up a bottle of wine and have it at the flop house after we eat."

At the Mission, they waited in line for their dinner ration of beans, bread, and coffee. Bobby almost lost his appetite completely as he nursed the food down.

The pillow was soft under his head at the flophouse.

The next morning, the manager awakened Bobby.

"Okay, your night is up. If you want to stay, it'll be four more bits."

"What time is it?"

"Eight o'clock—check-out time."

"Where's my friend?"

"Who knows? I'm not a baby sitter. You staying or not?"

"No, I don't have anymore money." Bobby tied his clothes up with a string, and slung the bundle over his shoulder.

*   *   *

On the sidewalk, Bobby began panhandling. It didn't take him long to get fifty cents.

"Say buddy, just enough for a cup of coffee?"

He crossed 31st Street and headed for the diner. On the way, he decided to grab a quick snort at a nearby bar.

His placed his four quarters on the bar, picked up the glass, and sipped his whiskey, exactly the way Sammy explained. He decided it was pretty good.

*   *   *

For the rest of the day, he panhandled a few more dollars, returned to the bar for a drink, then panhandled some more. As evening set in, he staggered to the Mission to have dinner.

*   *   *

The line was so long that by the time he reached the serving area, the Mission had run out of food, save for a few pieces of bread. He sat at a table, and dipped his bread in his neighbor's gravy when he thought he wasn't looking. But the guy caught him.

"New at this game, eh kid? Like a week, maybe?"

"Three days."

"What's your hang up?"

"You wouldn't believe me if I told you."

"You're kind of young to be in our business, kid. Say twenty-eight?"

"Twenty-seven."

"That's too young. Get back on the path, before it's too late. This is a hard life. At my age, it makes no difference one way or the other."

Bobby changed the subject. He yearned for a drink. "Say, Pop, where can I get a free drink?"

"Free?"

"Yes, I'm broke."

"Tell you what. Go to the corner of Houston and Bowery Streets. You'll see the boys gathered around; you can't miss them. Just tell them that Big Bart sent you. That will help you get a snifter."

"Hey, thanks, Pop. Maybe I'll help you someday."

"Sure, kid. Lots of luck."

*   *   *

The old guy was right. You couldn't miss the guys. They are some tough-looking dudes, Bobby thought. He had no fear—he was one of them now. He mentioned Bart's name to a guy who looked like someone important.

"He said you'd give me a drink.

"What do you have to throw in the pot?"

"Nothing right now, but I will."

He handed Bobby a bottle. One of the others protested. "Hey, we don't even know this guy! We should vote on it, right fellas?"

The leader looked at the protestor with fire in his eyes, "He knows Bart, don't he? That's number one. Number two, I'm in charge, and if anybody wants to make anything of it, just step up."

There were no takers.

The guy handed Bobby the bottle. "Here, take as much as you want. Remember, I'll be looking for a contribution from you."

"Sure, thanks." He brought the bottle to his lips and swallowed too much, too quickly. He felt as if he'd been struck by lightning. He couldn't catch his breath. The boys started laughing as the leader slapped him on the back a few times to get his color back.

Bobby tried to stand tall and show them he was capable of keeping up with them. He took another gulp and tried his best not to react. He passed the bottle back to the leader, who then passed it among the others before it got back to Bobby. After the third shot, his limbs began to tingle. He felt groggy. After the fourth one, he felt no pain at all.

He ended up sleeping in a shoemaker's doorway. For the next few days, Bobby lost even more weight from lack of food.

* * *

Four days later, he still had not contributed anything to the pot, so Bobby headed for 42nd Street to try his luck. Four hours later, he was still penniless. He went back to Bowery Street. There he saw five or six guys heading east toward Broadway and Pike.

"Where we headed?"

"The Manhattan Bridge."

"What for?"

"Are you kidding, or some kind a wise guy?"

"No, I'm not a wise guy; I'm new at this. I'm Bart's friend."

"Oh, okay. Hold onto this rag and do what we do."

On the bridge, they were cleaning car windshields for twenty-five to fifty cents when the drivers stopped for the traffic signal. Within two hours, Bobby had made enough to contribute toward his share of booze.

* * *

Bobby awoke the next morning cold and damp. His throat felt raw and he had difficulty swallowing. The booze no longer deadened the pain. Each day his condition worsened. At the Mission, breakfast was a waste of time. The coffee was too hot and the doughnuts too coarse to swallow. He developed the shakes as the pain increased.

After passing out, he awoke on the concrete floor of a jail cell.

"What happened?" he asked a familiar face.

"Vagrancy. They will let us out later."

Bobby crawled into a corner of the cell and tried to keep warm. As he coughed, he began spitting up blood. He broke into a cold sweat and his shakes became more intense. A guard sent for help. "Call for the wagon. Get him to the city hospital. He's ill."

*   *   *

The bright fluorescent ceiling lights reflected harshly off the white walls of the emergency room of the New York General Hospital. Once Bobby adjusted his vision, he saw a young doctor was standing over him.

"Welcome back, Mr. Smith. You gave us a good scare. We thought that we lost you several times. I'm Dr. Simons; you have been admitted to New York General Hospital. We call all our unknown guests Mr. Smith. Now what is your given name?"

Bobby turned his head toward the wall.

"Well, how do you like that for appreciation?"

Bobby still wouldn't respond.

"All right, have it your way. But you'll get a much-needed shower and shave." Dr. Simons called in an orderly. Bobby was given a shower, fed jell-o and broth, given medication, and finally put to bed.

*   *   *

Bobby was discharged wearing a clean pair of trousers, a clean shirt, and a sweater donated by the hospital staff. Unfortunately, he had to wear the same pair of shoes he wore when he had been admitted.

He shuffled out of the hospital and back onto to the street. He put his hands in his pockets to keep them warm. Inside were two five-dollar bills. He turned and saw Dr. Simons standing at the entrance, watching him.

*   *   *

He wasted no time getting back to Bowery and Houston. His friends hardly recognized him in his clean clothes. He endured their greetings and was given a bottle of white lightning. Bobby reached in his pocket, pulled out both five-dollar bills, and tossed one in the pot. Everyone gave him a good-natured cheer.

The leader took the other five-dollar bill. "Take him to the flop house and pay for ten nights. He'll be warm for a while."

*   *   *

Back at Bobby's old apartment, Mary was knocking at his door in a desperate attempt to reach him. Mr. Slade heard the commotion.

"Hold on, young lady. Do you want to knock down the door?"

Mary apologized and asked about Bobby.

"I'm sorry, but the apartment has been vacant for some time now."

"Do you have any idea where he might have gone?"

Slade felt sorry for Mary, but he explained that he had no idea where Bobby had gone. She took a card from her purse and handed it to him.

"If Bobby shows up, please contact me." She thanked him and left.

*   *   *

With each day, Bobby was getting accustomed to his new way of life. But he was also becoming rundown and looking much older. The clothes he wore were now too big for his thin frame, and his shoes were worn through the soles. He had to shuffle his feet so they would not slip off.

As the days and weeks went by, nothing could heal or repair the scar that Bobby wore in his heart. He felt he was not deserving of the bad breaks he had received in the past year. His fight was gone. Also gone was his hope to return to the real world. He was just tired. He seemed to be losing his faculties. The older members of the Bowery could see him deteriorating. They had seen it many times before. Yes, it was a shame; and he was a young man to boot. They tried one final time to talk Bobby into returning to society. Bobby simply asked for booze.

"It's a shame," said the oldest member of the Bowery. "If he lasts the winter, it'll be a miracle." The word was passed to keep a vigil on Bobby to make certain that he made it to the soup line. They even managed to get him a bunk at the Mission.

*   *   *

Eventually, curiosity took Bobby back to Broadway. His friends were amazed. For some reason, this journey was the only thing that seemed to perk up his spirits.

This night was no exception. While strolling Broadway, he managed to panhandle a quarter now and then.

"Bobby, Bobby is that you?" The voice seemed familiar to Bobby's ear, but he couldn't place it.

"Bobby, it's me—Mary." She grabbed him by the arm. "Come with me. I know it's you Bobby. Please talk to me."

Bobby shook her hand loose. By that time, those watching over Bobby surrounded Mary.

"Beat it, sister; leave him be." Mary stopped in her tracks, turned, and slowly walked away. She disappeared into the night.

Bobby wondered if he knew that person, but he couldn't be sure. He finally started his return trip to the Mission.

*   *   *

Bobby's health continued on its downward spiral. It was becoming more difficult for him to beg. His friends didn't think he would last more than three or four months without help—he was getting so bad that he would not leave the Mission. He sat on his bunk and stared blankly at the walls and ceiling. Those keeping watch over him had to feed him.

*   *   *

"Hey, gold-brick! Get off your ass! You can't make any money lying on the rack all day and all night. I leave you for a few weeks and whadda we get?" It was Sammy.

Bobby's body stiffened as he tried to place the voice. He turned slowly and looked up.

"Who are you?"

"Little Red Riding Hood, who did you expect? It's me, Sammy, your panhandling partner."

Bobby looked up and stared at Sammy. "Sure, sure we are buddies," he laughed. "Where's the booze?"

Sammy now realized that Bobby did not remember him. He motioned to the others to leave for a while. It was suppertime. Sammy had a bottle with just a swallow remaining. He placed the bottle to Bobby's lips; he finished it with one gulp.

Bobby looked at Sammy and motioned for more whiskey.

"If you got off your ass, we could go in town, make some money, and buy more whiskey. Whaddaya say, kid?"

Bobby sat back on his bunk and started rocking back and forth. He tried to hum. Sammy watched him with sadness. He continued talking to Bobby, hoping that he would snap out of it.

Meanwhile, the boys returned with a container of soup and crackers. They placed it on a small stool by Bobby's bunk. Bobby just looked at the soup.

"Now look here. I'm not like these bozos. You are going to feed yourself. You're not a baby."

Sammy picked up the container. After a moment, Bobby took it from him. He was barely able to hold it with two hands. Bobby managed to finish all the soup. He wiped his mouth and chin with his sleeve, smiled at Sammy, and lay down.

"Atta boy, kid; you're going to be just fine. Well, I can't make any money this way. I need to help get you back on your feet. Be a good kid and I'll see you later tonight. We'll have you back in good health in no time."

Bobby's physical and mental health continued to deteriorate despite Sammy's care. Sammy even gave him a bottle now and then. But it wasn't enough. Sammy finally realized that Bobby had given up.

CHAPTER 14

At midnight, Bobby became restless. He wanted to walk around Broadway. He managed to pick himself up, looked around to make certain that no one was watching, and quietly slipped out, staggering down Delancey Street. He just about made it to Lafayette but he was too weak. He headed back to the Mission.

Suddenly, he came upon a produce truck that had its tailgate down. Bobby leaped onto the tailgate, losing one shoe in the process.

Bobby jumped from the truck at 40th Street and limped toward 42nd.

The "night people" were out in force. Flamboyant couples out for a night on the town and fur-clad ladies decked out in all their finery gave him a wide berth. Bobby took a deep breath each time he passed a group of people.

Tears welled in his eyes. Passersby sneered at the sobbing, foul-smelling vagrant.

He walked several blocks, staring at the neon lights from the marquees of New York's finest theatres. In his confused state, he wondered aimlessly about the same streets over and over again.

"Mr. Shane? Mr. Bobby Shane, is that you?" It was Tommy Simms, the playwright.

"What? You talking to me, mister?"

"If you're Bobby Shane, I'm talking to you!"

"Do I know you?" he asked, straining to recognize the figure.

"How can you forget this ugly face, Mr. Shane? I didn't forget your face. I'm the show writer, remember?"

"Sure, sure I do." But he had no idea. "Wow, you're all spruced up, tuxedo and all. You getting married or something? Spare a dime?"

Bobby's friends did not interfere.

Tommy realized Bobby was in trouble.

He wrapped his arm under Bobby's for support, then flagged a cab. "Boyd Theater please."

*　　*　　*

Tommy helped Bobby out of the cab and asked the driver to wait. Tommy noticed people were laughing at them.

"Don't let them bother you, because you will have the last laugh, I assure you." He led Bobby toward the front of the theater. There he pointed to the marquee that read SIMMS AND SHANE PRESENT LOVE AND THE WORLD—Smash Hit Held over for the Fifteenth week!

Bobby stood like a statue, uncomprehending. "I don't understand."

"What is there to understand? You were my benefactor when I needed one. Our show is one of the greatest hits on Broadway. This is the fifteenth week, which means that you and I are partners, fifty-fifty. Your share has been held in escrow for you."

Bobby's eyes focused on his name on the marquee. For a second, he seemed to understand. His entire body began trembling.

With the driver's help, Tommy put Bobby back in the cab. "Madison Arms Hotel."

At the hotel, the lobby was unusually crowded. The manager offered his assistance. "Excuse me, Mr. Simms—is there something wrong?"

"No, nothing is wrong; except my friend here is very ill and will be spending some time with me. Send the hotel doctor to my apartment immediately."

Tommy continued to the elevator, practically carrying Bobby on his shoulders. "The hotel doctor is just temporary. I'll have a specialist examine you in the morning."

Tommy could not get his key from his pocket, so he rang the doorbell with his elbow. When the door was opened, Tommy spoke seriously. "George, not a word, do you understand?"

"Quite, sir."

"Good. Fill the tub with warm water, then help me get Mr. Shane cleaned up and into bed."

* * *

Bobby almost looked human again after the hot bath and shave. Once Bobby was in bed, Tommy had George prepare hot brandy. He tried to lift Bobby into a sitting position, placing pillows behind his back for support. Bobby was unable to sit up, so Tommy fed him the hot brandy with a spoon. Bobby coughed it up as fast as Tommy fed it to him. He soon fell into a deep sleep.

Tommy stood silent and looked at Bobby in astonishment. He ran his fingers through his hair.

"Where in the hell is that doctor?"

* * *

It was the wee hours of the morning when Dr. Williams arrived. He examined Bobby for ten minutes, then came out of the bedroom with an urgent look on his face.

"This man needs immediate medical attention. He is critically ill in an advanced stage of dehydration."

The paramedics wheeled him from the hotel room to a waiting ambulance. Intravenous fluid dripped into his arm, and an oxygen mask was strapped to his face.

A cool dawn was breaking as he was wheeled a short distance into the hospital's emergency unit and transferred to a gurney.

Tommy nervously paced the floor, anxiously awaiting word on Bobby's condition.

Finally, Dr. Shaw came to the waiting room and spoke to him.

"Mr. Shane is a very sick man. He has pneumonia. Fluid is rapidly filling both lungs. His liver is inflamed. His throat and larynx are in terrible condition. It appears as though he had throat surgery that didn't heal properly. He's lost some blood and seems to be bleeding internally. To make matters worse, it appears he does not have the will to live. At the moment, he has a fifty-fifty chance of surviving. That's all the information that I have at this time. After his admission, Dr. Grossman will be attending to him. He's already conducting more examinations. After his evaluation, he will prescribe the best treatment for Mr. Shane."

Later on, Dr. Grossman entered the waiting room and introduced himself. "We have a very sick man here. We are giving him high doses of antibiotics and pain medication to make him comfortable. In an hour or so, we will re-evaluate his conditions. Hopefully we will see progress in fighting his infection. The next twenty-four hours are crucial. If he doesn't respond to the treatment—"

Numb with disbelief, Tommy told the doctor, "I want the best for him; I don't care about the cost."

A nurse interrupted their conversation. The doctor excused himself and disappeared through the double doors.

*   *   *

Sammy walked the streets, looking for Bobby. He overheard a group of women at a bus stop who were talking about the morning paper's headline. One of the women showed the others the front-page article on Bobby Shane. Sammy poked his face into her newspaper. Agitated at the dirty smelly vagabond, the woman tossed her newspaper to the ground.

Sammy studied the photograph.

"I recognize this person." He read the caption: Bobby Shane Hospitalized, Condition Grave. "Well I'll be! That's him!"

He tossed the newspaper and headed for the hospital.

*   *   *

At the hospital, a swarm of tabloid reporters pushed their way to the information desk. Tommy saw an attractive woman talking to some of the reporters. He was mesmerized by her beauty and wondered who she was. She noticed Tommy staring at her and approached him.

"Hi, I'm Sheila Ross, a friend of Mr. Shane. Are you a member of his family?"

"No, but a good friend." He paused for a moment. "You're Sheila Ross, the actress! I knew I recognized you."

"What is Bobby's prognosis?"

"Really bad. The doctors have said the next twenty-four hours are critical. How did you know about Bobby's illness?"

"A radio news bulletin. I just completed a motion picture and decided to come to New York for a visit. I was listening to a music station when I heard the news about Bobby's illness."

Dr. Grossman approached them. "There's nothing more to tell you except that we're treating him with different medications and hoping for the best."

"How long 'til we know?" Tommy asked.

"Eight to ten hours."

"Thanks, Doc."

Suddenly, there was a ruckus in the hall. Tommy went to investigate and saw a hospital security guard confronting a shabbily dressed individual. Tommy figured this person might have been a friend of Bobby's.

He quickly intervened. "Oh, guard, I know him. I'll take care of things."

Sammy gave Tommy a puzzled look.

"It's all right," Tommy told him. "I have a feeling you know Bobby."

"How is my friend?" Sammy asked.

"No one can see him yet. They are still attending to him, so we must wait. We are on our way to have lunch. Care to join us?"

Surprised at the invitation, Sammy looked down at his clothes, and then looked at Tommy.

"You look just fine. Come with us."

* * *

At a nearby diner, each of them explained how they had met Bobby.

"Wow, I had no idea that my friend is a celebrity!" Sammy exclaimed.

Tommy scratched his chin. "I need to freshen up a bit. How about if we go to my place—I'm becoming self-conscious." He turned to Sammy. "If you like, we'll meet you back at the hospital in an hour or so."

* * *

Back at the hospital, there seemed to be no improvement in Bobby's condition. The waiting room was still a mass of reporters.

Sammy returned and joined Sheila and Tommy. Tommy grew impatient and decided to look in on his friend. It was difficult to recognize him through all the tubes and wires that were attached to Bobby's body. Edema swelled his face. Tommy returned to the waiting room.

*   *   *

Mary Rich's work was demanding. Most of the time she didn't mind working twelve hours a day and weekends; it took her mind off Bobby's illness. Even her mother's messages went unanswered.

She knew she had to visit Bobby. She informed her secretary that she was leaving for the day, then proceeded to the hospital.

*   *   *

Mary wasn't able to see Bobby right away, so she sat in the waiting room. She overheard Sheila and Tommy discussing Bobby.

"I'd like to introduce myself—I'm Mary Rich, Bobby's childhood friend."

Tommy and Sheila explained how they had come to know Bobby.

Mary then excused herself and walked toward Bobby's room hoping to see him. Nurse Beatrice smiled at Mary and told her it was all right for her to see him for ten minutes.

Mary was shocked at the sight of the man she loved since childhood. She held his hand in hers; he opened his eyes, smiled, and then closed them again.

*   *   *

Two hours later, Dr. Grossman approached Tommy.

"Mr. Simms, I am afraid that Mr. Shane is not responding. His condition is deteriorating, but we won't stop trying."

"Meaning what, Doc?"

"It looks as though Mr. Shane may not make it. I'm sorry."

"How long?"

"Six, maybe twelve hours."

Tommy, along with Mary, Sheila, and Sammy proceeded to Bobby's room. "Why in the world are you giving up?" Tommy whispered, stroking Bobby's hand

Bobby saw an apparition of Lester standing before him with his hand outstretched.

"Come with me, Bobby. It's time."

"Lessst, Lessst," Bobby moaned. He reached for Lester's hand, then took a deep breath. Bobby was now with his mother, father, and Lester.

Sheila cried hysterically. Tommy, with his hand on Bobby's, just stared at his prostrate body. A warm tear rolled down his cheek. But Mary didn't cry. She smiled as she took Bobby's hand in hers. Deep in her heart, she knew Bobby was at peace with his family.

*   *   *

The next morning, they gathered in Tommy's office to discuss Bobby's burial. Mary requested that Bobby be buried next to his parents. Tommy honored her request. He even agreed to cover all of the funeral costs.

Tommy then retrieved a dirty and crumpled envelope from his desk and handed it to Mary.

"Sammy found it where Bobby was living at the mission. He never got the chance to put it in the mail."

Mary took the letter in her hand, studied it, and then she tried to wipe it clean with her handkerchief. She slowly opened the envelope to find a one page letter from Bobby:

> My Dearest Mary:
>
> I find it difficult to write this letter because there are so many things that I want to say to you that I don't know where to begin. But I want to tell you how terribly sorry I am for not treating you the way I should have. I was a selfish and stupid person by thinking only of myself and forgetting who my real friends and loved ones were. I gave up the great times living in the old neighborhood: singing at weddings and special gatherings. I spent time away from you and our many friends for a short life in the fast lane instead of staying where I belonged—to live a happy and normal life at home.
>
> In closing, my only hope was to make it up to you. However, at the present time, my life is in disarray and I don't know the outcome."
>
> Love, Bobby

Mary put the letter back in the envelope, folded it, and placed it in her pocketbook. She turned to Tommy and thanked him.

Tommy then took a check from the desk drawer and offered it to Mary.

"This was to have been Bobby's first check. I'm sure that he would want you to have it and the monthly check thereafter.

She paused and then asked Tommy to deduct a percentage from the check each month and donate it to the Mission. "I'm sure Bobby would have liked, that."

*   *   *

There wasn't much fanfare for Bobby's arrival back home. A few fans waited at the airport, and a handful of local businesses placed Bobby's picture in their windows with token messages of farewell.

But for the funeral, the church was filled to capacity. Tommy and two of Bobby's best friends gave moving eulogies.

*   *   *

As the funeral procession arrived at the cemetery, a hard, whipping rain began to fall. These same conditions had been present at Lester's funeral. When the services were over, everyone left for the luncheon except Mary, who sat at the gravesite alone while Tommy waited in the car.

Mary stared at the casket and reminisced about the good times she and Bobby had shared while growing up. When she stood up to leave, she saw an apparition of Bobby. He was seventeen-years-old, singing at one of the many weddings he had attended. She took a rose, kissed it, and placed it on Bobby's casket. At that moment, the rain stopped, and the sun shone brightly. Mary looked up and saw a rainbow arcing across the sky. She took one last look at the gravesite, turned, and walked toward the car waiting for her.

www.ingramcontent.com/pod-product-compliance
Lightning Source LLC
Chambersburg PA
CBHW050308260626
47156CB00005B/1710